Praise for

Crossing
The Border

"With little hope in her homeland, one seeks to look elsewhere. *Crossing the Border* is a collection of short stories from Ukrainian writer Ksenia Rychtycka as she tells many stories surrounding Ukraine, as well as the world around it, describing characters facing events in the nation's recent history and their personal journeys. With a good dose of humor and insight into the lives of Ukrainians, *Crossing the Border* is a must for any international fiction collection."

— *Midwest Book Review*
(Reviewer's Choice)

"One of the strongest characters in this anthology is *Babtsia*. The image of the strong and competent Ukrainian grandmother caring for the emotional and spiritual needs of future generations is skillfully portrayed by Rychtycka."

—Myra Junyk,
Nash Holos Ukrainian Radio

"The bottom line is that all the stories examine what it is to be human and that is always what makes a book compelling to me. I know little about Ukraine and its people. Author Rychtycka let me see the intimate part of Ukrainian history, its culture and community. This is an excellent collection from Rychtycka and I look forward to her future works."

— Lit Amri,
Readers' Favorite (Five-Star Review)

"Ksenia Rychtycka weaves her characters with dignity, compassion, and strength in *Crossing the Border*. Blending history and ethnicity, each story delivers universal human emotions with an amazing voice. The reader is captivated, anticipating each turn of the page."

— Susan Noe Harmon, author,
Under the Weeping Willow

"*Crossing the Border* takes the homegrown American into the world of a country that is nothing like our own. Ksenia Rychtycka guides us through that world in her short stories to our country with the hope that we, too, can see the world through her eyes."

— Linda Hudson Hoagland, author,
Lindsay Harris Murder Mystery Series

"Rich characters, haunting images, compelling stories . . . *Crossing the Border* is a must-read."

— Tammy Robinson Smith, author,
Emmybeth Speaks

KSENIA RYCHTYCKA

Crossing The Border

stories

Jan-Carol
Publishing, Inc

"every story needs a book"

Crossing the Border
Ksenia Rychtycka

Published October 2012
Second Edition Published August 2014
Third Edition Published May 2019
Little Creek Books
Imprint of Jan-Carol Publishing, Inc
Copyright © Ksenia Rychtycka

ISBN: 978-1-939289-01-8
Library of Congress Control Number: 2012918157

You may contact the publisher at:
Jan-Carol Publishing, Inc
PO Box 701
Johnson City, TN 37605
E-mail: publisher@jancarolpublishing.com
Website: jancarolpublishing.com

For Daria Melnykowycz Rychtycka,
mother and poet extraordinaire

"40 Days" is dedicated to the memories of
Atena Pashko and Vyacheslav Chornovyl

Author's Note

I have used the Ukrainian transliterations for place names such as Kyiv versus Kiev, Dnipro versus Dnieper, etc. A glossary of the italicized Ukrainian and Greek words can be found at the end of the book.

Acknowledgements

The birth of this book has been years in the making, and I'd like to thank everyone who inspired and supported me over the years:

The Columbia College Chicago Fiction Writing Department with its unique Story Workshop approach, originated by John Schultz. Special thanks to Randy Albers and Andy Allegretti, in whose workshops it all started so many years ago;

Laura Bernstein-Machlay and Dorene O'Brien, for many years of friendship, unflagging support, insight and endless bouts of spot-on critiquing;

Little Creek Books/Jan-Carol Publishing for making my dream come true. Thanks to Janie Jessee, Tammy Robinson Smith, Sloane Trentham Uphoff, and Tara Sizemore;

My mother who exposed me to the power of storytelling at a young age; my sister Tamara and my brother Nestor, for always standing with me; Vera Sirota for her boundless enthusiasm and creative suggestions; and Oles and Mark Slywynsky for their reliance and wholehearted support. Although my father passed away many years ago, I am grateful for the literary works he left behind and the joy he expressed in my earliest writings;

And finally, Volodya and Lina Horobchenko, for filling my life with love and encouraging me to follow my passions.

I am also very grateful to the editors who published the following stories in these journals:

Twenty Years After The Fall (Parlor City Press), "Homecoming"

Driftwood: A Literary Journal of Voices From Afar, "40 Days"

Wisconsin Review, "The Artist"

Foliage, Short Story Quarterly, "Whitewashed Sojourn"

Emergence, "Babtsia"

River Poets Journal, "Tricks of the Eye"

The MacGuffin, "The Bell Tower"

Yellow Medicine Review, "Crossroads"

The Dalhousie Review, "Orange in Bloom"

And the uniqueness of every moment
seeks the path from pain to a pearl.

— Lina Kostenko
(translated from Ukrainian by Michael M. Naydan)

Hope is definitely not the same thing as optimism.
It is not the conviction that something will turn out well,
but the certainty that something makes sense,
regardless of how it turns out.

— Vaclav Havel

Table of Contents:

Homecoming

Summer 1990

Vera hasn't seen her cousin Stefko in 47 years, but when the train carrying her from Budapest finally crosses the border into Ukraine, all she can think about is mountains—mountains that are lush and green and well-suited to hide a plenitude of graves. Vera's brother Maxym is buried in one of those unmarked graves.

Stefko, in the meantime, awaits her in their hometown of Krynytsia. The town is named after the abundant mineral springs that once dotted the countryside like flowers, but Stefko has already warned Vera not to expect things to be the way she remembers them.

"The springs have all dried out," he wrote her in his last letter. "The river where you taught me how to swim has shriveled into a creek, and you won't recognize your old house. It's still standing, but now there are two families that live there, and no one is too concerned about the upkeep."

Vera has that letter in her purse. She read it at least a dozen times during the overnight transatlantic flight from Detroit to Germany and then during the transfer to Budapest where she joined the tour group, still the easiest way to gain entry into any of the Soviet-bloc countries. She isn't the only woman who travels alone in the group, which is mostly made up of people like her: immigrants who fled Ukraine some 50 years earlier and who are now flocking back, not unlike migratory birds, Vera thinks, returning to familiar ground.

Even though she's thought about visiting her homeland for decades and imagined what it'd be like to slip incognito past all the barriers and Soviet bureaucracy, Vera can't quite believe her luck. Last month while celebrating her 58th birthday in Michigan, Ukraine declared its sovereignty from the Soviet Union, and now Vera is convinced it's only a matter of time before independence is as real as the Ukrainian visa stamped in her brand-new U.S. passport.

Her cousin isn't convinced about any of this. The wording in his letters—succinct and cautious, as though someone was standing over his shoulder, analyzing every stroke of the pen—provides Vera with more information than he probably realizes. "Let's wait and see," is Stefko's favorite phrase, and he sprinkles it liberally throughout his letters, responding in this way to most of Vera's questions. Vera wants to know everything—from prospects about independence to whether she'll be able to venture freely throughout the country without benefit of an official escort. Until recently, Vera had only received one letter from her cousin in all the years of separation, and before she even opened it, Vera knew that Teta Nelya, who was Stefko's mother, was dead. That was five years ago, but Stefko hadn't answered any of Vera's ensuing letters until six months ago when a postcard unexpectedly arrived.

"Dear Verochka," he wrote. "Your cousin is alive and well and wonders if you'll consider visiting him now that some of the old restrictions have eased up a bit."

In spite of everything, Vera didn't hesitate in writing back. "I'm coming home, Stefko."

* * *

Stefko sits in his den and studies the picture Vera sent in her last letter. His cousin looks beautiful; not a day over 45, if even that. In the photograph, she is wedged between her two daughters, Katrusia and Maya, and they're standing on the front porch of a big house with their arms wrapped around one another. The house looks well-kept, and it is constructed from neat blocks of dark-red brick. Even the shutters have been painted a burgundy color to match the stone. Both women resemble their father who's been dead for close to 25 years now, but they've got Vera's smile, and Stefko wonders if they're upbeat, impatient and fearless like her or if they've taken after their father's side of the family, which Stefko doesn't know too much about. Over the years, Vera wrote letters and sent family pictures to his mother, so Stefko has been kept up-to-date on her life to some degree.

Vera is still tall and slender, the way he remembers her. Even though they're the same age, in childhood he'd been more like a kid brother and always let her take the lead, which inevitably led them into more trouble than Stefko would have thought up on his own. Vera's brother, Maxym, who was six years older used to tease Stefko about it, but back then Stefko was shy around the other kids. Vera was the one who always accepted him.

Not for the first time, Stefko wonders how his life would have turned out if he'd made it to the West. Here in his own country, he has prided himself on being a good communist. It wasn't a decision he'd aspired to initially, but after half of his family was torn away from him in one way or another, it had been the only sensible response. When Stefko was nine, his father died of a heart attack. Two years later, Vera fled with her parents to the West just days before the Red Army occupied their town and all of the surrounding region. Maxym never made it back after he joined the partisans, so Stefko had been left to grow up alone under his own mother's cautious ministrations.

"Are you still holed up in here?" Marichka asks, opening the door and waving her hands at her husband as though he's a child who needs to be shooed out into the fresh air. "I've asked Oksana to stop by and clean up while I run out to the bazar."

Stefko stares at Marichka like he hasn't heard a word she's said.

"Are you daydreaming again? You've got to snap out of it. Your American cousin will think you've gone daft in your old age."

"Do you remember when we first met?" Stefko asks. "Do you remember how hard the snow was falling? It seemed as though it would never end, and nobody could talk about anything else."

"I nearly broke my leg on the sidewalk," Marichka says. "As it was, I spent days hobbling around after that. And you were so busy treating all the patients who were coming in that you barely had a chance to look out the window. So what's so special about the weather all of a sudden?" Marichka rests her hands on her hips and sniffs the air. "You haven't started smoking again, have you? You always get maudlin after a few cigarettes."

"Look," Stefko says. He wants her to know it's not the cigarettes or even staring at Vera's photograph for the last half-hour. His mother had never been crazy about Marichka, but he recalls how happy Marichka had been in the clinic when he treated her in spite of the pain in her leg. It was the first time he'd been so nervous about treating a patient since his first days as a doctor, but Marichka's smiles and jokes about her clumsiness made him feel as though they'd known each other for years. Stefko remembers how magical the day seemed with its unceasing snow and how young and buoyant he'd felt as if he was finally gaining something in his life instead of losing it. He wants to explain about the snow, about the joy of seeing Vera again, but then

3

he looks up at his wife, who is intent on getting the house cleaned and the groceries purchased, and Stefko shrugs.

"Don't forget the champagne," he says. "And maybe some red *Muscat* too."

* * *

Going back home is something Vera has thought about since she was eleven years old, and she and her parents had stepped out the front door into the midst of chaos. By then, she'd grown used to seeing soldiers and hiding at a moment's notice or slipping into the abandoned wine cellar at the far end of their property. After five years of wartime occupation when both the Soviets and the Nazis took their turns, it was apparent in the summer of 1944 that instead of the liberation they'd all been expecting, only Soviet reoccupation was at hand. So Vera and her parents started walking west; first to the neighboring village of Soloma where, for the price of some pearls, they were able to get a ride on a horse-drawn wagon to the border of Hungary and then through Hungary to Austria where they had ended up behind barbed wire at a refugee internment camp. Vera shakes her head, for the moment at least. She didn't want to think about the gunfire and shelling or the time they'd cowered under an oak tree while warplanes dropped bombs over their heads. All she wants to focus on are the Carpathian Mountains as she sits there in the dark and waits for dawn to break. She knows they're getting closer now that the train is moving again. Vera had waited for six hours at the Ukrainian border while mechanics changed the wheels to fit the special tracks Stalin had ordered after the war ended to ensure no Western country could invade the Soviet Union through the railway system.

Vera grew up in the foothills of these mountains, and for as long as she can remember, she has dreamed about seeing them at least one more time. When first light comes, she leaves her compartment and heads for a window in the corridor. She stands there, unable to take her eyes from the view. The lush slopes skim past her window, goats amble along as if on a Sunday stroll and houses are bedecked in flowers. Everything appears so surreal and welcoming at the same time that Vera doesn't know where to fix her eye. When she finally swallows her wonder at being here at all, the train speeds up and accelerates in a mad surge, as though knowing it has to make up for years of lost time.

Vera doesn't know how long she's been standing at the window, but she doesn't think anything of it until one of the train attendants walks past her for the fifth or sixth time. She smiles at him, and he tips his cap in response. He's a young man, younger than either of her daughters, and apparently he wants to talk, because a minute later he's standing at her elbow.

She shifts away a bit apprehensively. She had been warned about talking to strangers—this was still the Soviet Union after all.

"Say, I was wondering if you'd exchange some money for me? Dollars for local currency," he says. "I'll give you a better rate than the official exchange."

Vera hesitates. She had been told it was illegal to exchange money on the black market since the government didn't want locals making a profit for themselves.

"No, I don't think so," she says.

"Come on," he insists. "You'll be doing me a favor."

"It's illegal, right?"

"Who's going to ask any questions? You're American. No one will bother you."

"I'm sorry." Vera feels guilty for disappointing him but doesn't want to create any problems for herself at the very start of her trip.

"You Americans are all the same," he says as his coaxing tone unexpectedly slides into anger. "You won't lift a finger to help anyone else."

"What are you talking about? And by the way, I was born here, just like you," she says, but he has already walked away from her, muttering under his breath.

Vera stands there, wanting to erase his sudden anger from her mind. Does he even know anything about Americans or living in the United States? Yes, her new homeland has been very good and welcoming to her, but did this stranger have any idea how hard it'd been, too? He probably believes that money can ease anything, soothe any wound and right every wrong. Only, there hadn't been any money for Vera or her husband, Yarema, whom she'd met in the refugee camp after the war. The only money they had slipped into their fingers and then slid right out again before they could even count it. Vera thought it would be that way only in the beginning before she learned how to speak English and got her teaching degree. She believed that while she worked the cafeteria line of the local hospital during the early morning shift and then cleaned houses in her off-hours. At first it was just to survive the early years, and then it'd been to survive alone, she and the girls, without Yarema. She hadn't completed her teaching degree until long after her husband died and left her with two little girls and even less money.

Vera thinks of all the words she could have said to the young attendant, but then she shakes her head and turns back to the window, her eyes soaking up the remaining scenery like the final scenes of a beloved movie.

* * *

By the time the train pulls into Krynytsia, Stefko has smoked half a pack of cigarettes while pacing up and down the road in front of the *vokzal*. Volodya, his government-appointed driver who usually ferries him across town without comment, has offered him coffee, poppyseed *bulochky* that some old *babusias* are selling inside the station and, in desperation to get Stefko to relax, his own pack of cigarettes.

"Don't say a word to Marichka," Stefko warns him before he continues his frenzied walk, cigarette in hand.

The train stops before Stefko plods up the stairs and waits near the entryway. He lets the passengers edge past him before he shoulders his way down the aisle. He finally sees Vera two cars down, and he pauses to catch his breath. Stefko wants to make a good impression, but Vera spots him in the same instant that he stops to wipe his face. There's no time to catch a breath or think of a profound remark; no time to say any of the words he's rehearsed in his mind; no time to do anything but throw his arms around Vera and burst out laughing or crying, whichever comes first.

At first, they don't talk much; not until they make their way off the train and Volodya safely stows Vera's large suitcases in the trunk of the car. And then the words won't stop, and they're like two children caught chattering in the middle of the night—each trying to get as many words in as possible.

"If only the girls could have come too…" Stefko says.

"I want to see the school. It's still standing, isn't it?" Vera says.

"You look wonderful."

"And Dovbush's *skelia* where we used to jump off the rocks…"

Finally they pause, and Stefko sees that Vera's eyes glint like a young girl's. She looks refreshed, seemingly unfazed by the long journey, and not for the first time, Stefko thinks that he looks old with his balding head and saggy jaw.

"It wasn't easy," he says unexpectedly, surprising himself as much as Vera. He hopes that his words will make up for his sad state of appearance.

"But you'll see that I've done alright for myself and my family. Our Bohdan's a dentist and lives in Kyiv now. Their place is only a five-minute walk from the *Dnipro* river. His wife loves to decorate so much, the place

6

resembles a museum. They've got a house full of furniture imported from Italy and beautiful custom-made oak floors." Stefko shakes his head. "It's not easy to get a four-room flat like that, mind you, but his father-in-law's an important man with connections."

"Is that so?" Vera cuts in. Her voice is loud, but when Stefko tries to catch her eye, Vera turns away from him and stares out the window.

"I want to see my old house," she says as her voice drops almost to a whisper.

Stefko waits for her to say more. He wants to tell her how proud he is that Bohdan has made a successful career in the capital city hundreds of miles away from where he grew up. Of course, Bohdan had the savvy to marry a girl with good connections. Without Halyna, or more importantly her father, Bohdan's career would have advanced at a slower pace. Stefko wants to ask Vera if things operate the same way in America; if having the right connections is tantamount to being successful. He leans forward, but before he can formulate any questions into words, Vera stops him with a question of her own.

"All those years," she says. "Couldn't you ever write?"

Vera looks directly at him, only this time it's Stefko who turns away.

* * *

Stefko clenches and unclenches his fingers while Vera waits. She is immediately remorseful as she remembers how fearful he was as a child.

"Teta was a good letter writer," she says, unable to watch her cousin play with his hands any longer. "She'd write me about your vacations, your patients, even the dogs Bohdan would rescue and you'd inevitably take in."

"It probably took you hours to get through her letters," Stefko says after a pause. He then points out the library and town square through the car window. By the time the car grinds to a halt, they are both laughing at two small girls pushing a beleaguered puppy in a baby carriage right outside Stefko's house.

Marichka must have waited at the window, because she's out by the car before they even open the door. She looks Vera over from head to toe and engulfs her in an embrace. She then leads her through the house as though they're in a marathon while a clock ticks down the time. Blond and boisterous is all that Vera takes in before she is called upon to admire the spacious rooms that contain hand-painted goose-size *pysanky*, carved woodwork and sunburst-colored hand-woven rugs. Every piece spells elegance and power,

7

and Vera is dutifully impressed. She can see that Marichka is pleased with her reaction, and by the time Stefko trails in after them, Marichka has linked arms with Vera almost as if it is her own long-lost sister who has finally made her way home.

* * *

It doesn't take Vera long to confirm that inside Stefko's house, it's Marichka who makes all the decisions. Marichka is an interior decorator, professional chef and personal advisor all in one. She has organized Vera's itinerary for the first five days of her visit, and Vera can see why Teta Nelya's enthusiasm for her daughter-in-law had remained tepid over the years.

"She organizes every detail of their vacations, their social outings and even how much time Stefko should spend on a phone call," Teta Nelya had once complained in a letter to Vera, although she conceded that Marichka was good for him and kept Stefko from sliding into depression as he was sometimes apt to do.

For the past five days, Vera's been treated to tablefuls of Marichka's culinary delights—everything from *pyrizhky* and green *borsch* to lasagna-like treats stuffed with liver. There is no question that Marichka is an impeccable cook. But after yesterday's meal of fish *studenets* topped off by honey torte, Vera pushed back her chair, thanked Marichka and told her the elaborate meals had to stop. Marichka agreed but then this morning called Vera to a breakfast of crepes and buckwheat oatmeal, all delivered with a list of possible plans for the day. Vera doesn't say a word until Stefko joins them, suddenly realizing that they haven't had any opportunity to simply be alone.

"Take me to my old house," she says, looking at her cousin. Before Marichka can offer to come along or suggest any alternatives, Vera leans over and squeezes Stefko's hand.

"We haven't had much time to just catch up. I want to see the old neighborhood and look up some of our friends."

Stefko and Marichka look at each other, and then Marichka nods.

"I could use some time for myself," she says. She turns her head and then glances back at Vera. "But beware of old friends, Verochka. Sometimes it's best to revel in the memories."

* * *

It's not far to the old neighborhood, but as they walk down the narrow road, it's easy to see that Stefko's house, located in the center of town, is one

8

of the nicer ones. Vera usually doesn't pay great attention to details. Her daughters have even on occasion accused her of having a dreamy nature, but here, back in the country she'd left as a child, details have become vital. The trip's brought everything into focus, such as the fact that Stefko has his own chauffeur while Teta Nelya had never moved from their old home with an outhouse in the backyard and no running water inside. Stefko had told her his mother refused to move, but Vera can't help thinking about it now that the houses look more and more worn down the farther they walk from the center.

As they get nearer to her childhood home, Vera scours the landscape and searches for a familiar bend in the road, a sight of the old school or a glimpse of a familiar face, but they reach the house before Vera can connect anything of the present with her past.

Surrounded by unkempt grass and weeds, the house looks forlorn, just as Stefko had warned her in his letter. Vera remembers when her grandfather and father had built the house together as she stares at the brown peeling paint. They'd been so proud when it was finished and invited all the neighbors over for a party that lasted close to a week. Vera and Stefko had turned the house into their personal playground, playing the game of Ukrainians against Tartars, or more appropriately, Ukrainian against Tartar. Vera was usually cast in the role of Tartar, and both of them danced and stomped down the wooden hall leading from one end of the house to the other. Maxym, six years older, had only laughed when they'd asked him to join in.

"Enough," Vera's mother would finally yell in the midst of creaking floorboards and squeals of laughter. "Outside." She would clap her hands vigorously and, taking each of them by the back of their necks, would shoo them out the door. Vera still remembers the feel of her mother's hands, soft and silky and smelling of sweet roses.

"Mama and I never found out how Maxym died," Stefko says as he interrupts her thoughts. "The details, I mean. We're pretty sure he was killed and buried in the Carpathians though."

"My parents never got over not knowing what happened to him," Vera says. "Especially Mama. She kept waiting for some word from him or about him, even years later."

Vera doesn't want to admit it to Stefko, but Maxym had been her mother's favorite, or at the very least they had understood each other in a way that Vera and her mother never could.

Stefko shakes his head. "It was a hopeless cause, fighting against the Nazis and the Red Army at the same time. They didn't stand a chance."

"Don't say that." Vera looks at her cousin as her hands shake. She is surprised at her own reaction. "They were fighting for freedom. Is that what you told Bohdan? That Maxym died for nothing?"

Inexplicably, Stefko moves away from Vera, and that's when the realization hits her.

"You never told your own son that Maxym was a partisan, did you?" she asks. "Just like you never wrote me. You were afraid to lose your position."

"No, Vera," Stefko says. "I was simply afraid."

* * *

Stefko knows what they all think about him. Those childhood friends Vera mentioned at the dining room table were now running forward up the road to greet Vera, but were in no hurry to look him in the eye. Valia and Pavlo Ferchuk had attended school with Vera and Stefko and were now married. Valia finally steps forward and greets Stefko with a formal *Dobriy dyen*. It's more than what he gets from Pavlo, who merely bobs his head in greeting.

In the excitement of Vera's arrival, their unenthusiastic reception hardly matters. Although in some small, inexplicable way, Stefko is annoyed. He helped his own as much as he could, but he couldn't help everyone. Yes, there were a few times when he'd provided some information to the authorities. A few people even blamed him for ruining their careers, but Stefko hadn't been given a choice. He either had to save himself or save others, and in the end he had picked his family and gone to sleep with a clear head. The people he grew up with couldn't forgive him for that; the ones who'd stayed put on their little plots of land with the same mindsets they'd been born with. They only had themselves to blame for their misfortunes. So he smiles at Pavlo and Valia, and before long, he chats along with the others, conversing and smiling, and the whole time he wonders how quickly he can get Vera to leave.

* * *

The encounter with their old classmates is still on Stefko's mind the next day. They'd only managed to get away from Pavlo and Valia when Vera promised to stop by for dinner later that week. Vera will have to attend the dinner on her own since Stefko has no intention to pretend a camaraderie neither he nor the Ferchuks feel.

He'll make some excuse to Vera, but Stefko doesn't think she'll push the issue. Ever since she confronted him, there's been a subtle shift in the way they look at each other. But he smiles at her when she walks into the room and settles into a chair next to him.

"Tell me what it was like for you after we left," Vera says.

Stefko looks at her before he shakes his head. "Your family wasn't even gone a day before the neighbors were in the house, carting away the furniture, taking down the curtains and folding up the linens. Mama couldn't do much to stop them, but she salvaged what she could. The neighbors were the least of our worries once the new officials started interrogating Mama. I never saw her cry or lose her composure, but she lost about 40 pounds in the span of a few weeks." Stefko wipes his brow before he continues.

"She was sure we'd be sent to the labor camps along with most of the other villagers, but somehow they allowed us to stay. For a long time, we never spoke of any of you, even when we were alone."

Vera sits in silence, then moves forward unexpectedly, resting her head against her cousin's.

Stefko closes his eyes, wanting to prolong the moment as long as he can.

"Tato kept telling us we'd be back," Vera finally says and pulls away. "Every Christmas Eve he'd say that we'd be celebrating the next year back in our old house together with you and Teta. Finally one year, he just stopped saying it. But I don't know when he really stopped believing it."

"They were right to leave."

"You know Tato was a teacher," Vera says. "He'd already been arrested before."

"We all have to make our choices," Stefko says.

Vera looks up at her cousin. That pleading look in his eyes hasn't changed in 47 years, and Vera knows this is how she will always remember Stefko.

* * *

Vera's been in Ukraine for two weeks now, and lately her two daughters have been phoning every few days.

"Maybe they're afraid you won't go back," Stefko joked, just yesterday. "Of course, you couldn't give up your grand life there, could you?"

"You don't know what you're talking about Stefko," Vera had said and let it go at that.

Vera sits in the kitchen, sipping her coffee and waits for Stefko to come in so she can tell him her plans. In the morning, she will take her bags, leave

11

her cousin behind and head for the train station. In a couple of days she will rejoin the tour group, but for now, Vera wants to get to know this country of hers that's right on the brink of a new order. She wants to go to the highest peak in the Carpathian Mountains and plant a cross made of colorful flowers, just like the ones she's seen for all the freedom fighters on local roads. They usually drive by them without stopping, but yesterday Vera made Stefko stop the car while she took some pictures. She knows he's still afraid; afraid of things going back to the way they were and afraid of them staying the same, but in the end, Vera knows that the only steps to be taken are her own.

* * *

It's a bright summer morning, and there's not a cloud in the sky when Vera takes a last look at her childhood home in Krynytsia. She's alone this time, but the sun is as warm as it was 47 years earlier when she'd walked between her parents. Vera had been sullen because they wouldn't let her take Sirka along with them on the road. The cat had ran into the neighbor's yard, and before Vera could track her down, her parents pleaded and yelled at her, saying there was no time to lose. The cat went missing, just like her brother and thousands of others.

It's a nice house with a strong foundation in spite of its peeling exterior, Vera decides as she turns away, built to withstand even the many years of neglect it'd been subjected to.

Vera walks away, bending to the ground only one time to pick up a burnt orange pebble that is buried in the roadside past the boundaries of her home.

40 Days

The last time Luba saw her husband alive, he joked about the color of his suits in the same way he joked about his enemies—laughing, always laughing, as if a boisterous chuckle could fell death threats by the very audacity of its sound. Luba had wanted him to wear the dark suit for his campaign trip to the communist-oriented South, where support for a political prisoner-and-poet-turned-politician seemed about as absurd as buying vegetables from the contaminated zone north of Kyiv.

"A presidential candidate has to look distinguished," Luba told Roman. "You've got to convince them a former dissident can be a good president too."

"I'll wear the tan suit," Roman answered, waving away her words with a grin. "I'm not ready for the coffin yet."

And then Roman grabbed Luba close, lifted her by her waist and swung her around in circles until she fell laughing against his chest, Roman's fingers stroking her hair long after the laughter subsided.

* * *

Today is her husband's funeral. Six days after he refused his wife's request to dress in black, Luba has no choice but to remove another dark suit from the closet, iron it so carefully that the pleats stiffen, as crisp as the tone in her voice when she answers the phone, and Oles, Luba's stepson and Roman's son, tells her that the police investigation into Roman's death will take weeks at the very least.

"The rumor is they want the investigation to look solid," Oles says.

"Brakes going out on a brand-new Toyota?" Luba asks. "They can't claim it was an accident. Everyone knows the roads were dry that night."

"I told him this campaign was a crazy idea," Oles says. "All those years when I was growing up, he was in the labor camps, and now he'll miss his grandson's childhood too."

"He couldn't just sit idly by," Luba says.

Oles doesn't respond, but Luba knows what he's thinking: *She should have talked to Roman.* As if anyone could have prevented Roman from campaigning, even if she'd agreed to try.

"Oles," Luba's voice trembles. "You know that no one could have stopped him." But Oles is hanging up the phone, telling her he has to go, and he'll call her later. Before she can say anything else, the line goes dead.

* * *

Luba's been to many funerals in her life, but her husband's funeral at St. Nicholas Cathedral in the center of Kyiv seems more like a gathering of the masses than the typical affair. As the black hearse weaves its way past city blocks filled shoulder to shoulder with people, Luba stares out the window. She takes in the wide concrete buildings, the chestnut trees that have unexpectedly burst into bloom a few weeks early and all the wood barriers closing off the streets near the Cathedral. Buses are lined up, bumpers touching, parked erratically on the edges of the cracked sidewalks, and Luba can see by the signs in their windows that people came from all parts of the country.

"You see, darling," Luba whispers to herself. "They've all come to pay their respects."

Next to her in the hearse, Luba's older sister, Marusia, who'd taken the overnight express train from Lviv and arrived only a few hours earlier, pats Luba's hand.

"There wasn't an empty seat on the train last night," Marusia says. "Not even one."

Inside the immense Cathedral whose ceilings rise high to the sky, Luba feels the hot breath of friends and strangers against her neck. Their eyes look deeply into hers as if seeking some sort of solace or perhaps even a promise of retribution. Luba turns away from the questions mirrored in their faces, the awkward shrugs and the sympathetic nods and unexpectedly finds herself face to face with the president of her country. He is hardly taller than herself as he holds out his hand, mouthing sympathies, sweating noticeably in the stifling heat. Even through her black veil, Luba can sense the looks of disapproval cast his way. The looks around her are shrill with accusation, but Luba accepts the president's condolences just as she accepts condolences from the leaders of all the other political parties—the graying men and the

16

outspoken women—many of whom Roman had adamantly opposed.

Murder is the first word out of Oles' mouth once the funeral is over, and they are back at the apartment where Roman and Luba lived. There are about 20 people who have come over, bearing plates of *kanapky*, chicken and an assortment of beet and potato salads. It's traditional during *pomynky* to share stories about the person who's left them behind, but this time there's no room for any happy memories to shake away the somber mood.

"It's murder, I tell you." Oles bangs his fist on the table, his dark hair falling over his eyes. "And the order had to come from the top," he says, searing the room full of people with a look of fury.

Silence falls around the table with some of the guests nodding their heads in assent. In the past, Luba was always surprised how her stepson bore no resemblance to his father. While Roman was short and wiry, his son looms well over six feet tall and is as stocky as Roman was slender. But today, his grief is so outspoken that Luba can't help being reminded of his father. Roman's passion, once ignited, swept through obstacles in his path like a runaway elephant, oblivious to any attempts to stop the onslaught.

"Did you notice how they tried to keep the people away?" Marusia asks. "The police formed a human chain and wouldn't even let the old *babusias* in. 'It's too crowded; we have to keep the order,' was all they'd say."

"It's nothing to do with order," Oles says, rising from his chair. The edge of his hand accidentally sweeps a plate of food onto the floor. And even though he's had little to drink, Oles stumbles, eyes blurring and falls onto the red and white *kilim* covering the hardwood floor. In the 20 years she's been married to Roman, Luba has never seen her stepson lose his composure, but when she rushes to Oles' side and murmurs words of reassurance, he pushes her away with a look of confusion. The two of them stop and stare at one another; two people who have lost the one man binding them to one another, and for a second amid hesitation, their eyes lock. Then Oles looks away, and Luba steps back, her hands shaking at her sides.

* * *

When Luba was born, her parents named her after the Ukrainian word for love. *Lubov. Moya Luba. Lubochka.* Every letter Roman had ever written Luba started out with a different variation of her name.

Luba sits in their bedroom and sifts through the stack she's collected over the past 20 years. While Oles is calling daily press conferences, Luba can do

17

nothing more than walk through the apartment, waiting for a breath of warm air against her ear (hadn't he always whispered to her, even in the middle of the night when he thought she was asleep?) or the sound of footsteps in an empty room—anything to convince her she hasn't been completely left behind. Three weeks since they've buried Roman, and there's been no word from the police about the investigation. Luba knows this only because Marusia has been staying with her and fielding all the phone calls. The newspapers keep piling up on the kitchen table, but Luba barely glances at the headlines. She already knows all the conjectures and theories about Roman's death. From the communists who've hung on to their seats in the parliament to the current president whose fast dance with corruption is no longer a state secret, Roman's death appears to have paved the way for easy victory in next year's elections.

"They might argue about who's behind it," Luba tells her sister. "But no one believes it was an accident."

As Roman's widow, Luba is on the hot list for interviews. So far, she's turned down every single one of them and has instead focused on Roman's love letters that fill an entire drawer in her dresser. Luba's kept them all, the short notes that start off with a poem and end with a pencil drawing; the long letters that cover every square inch of paper, words crawling up margins in disarray. Once, on the back of a theatre program, Roman had even drawn a sketch of the Saint Sophia Cathedral, complete with the kiosk booth in front, where the two of them had gawked at images of saints plastered next to postcards of Soviet monuments and city vistas on the glass front of the booth.

Roman was good at noticing details like that. It was something Luba would tease him about; how he'd remember what tie a certain writer wore at a dinner; what song was playing over the loudspeaker when they'd kissed for the first time on Khreshatyk Boulevard while waiting for the metro; and what promises certain politicians made only to later deny they'd ever spoken those words aloud. Roman remembered details as if they were etched in glitter across a bare table. He told Luba it had been the only way he'd been able to write his poems during his 15 years in the labor camps—he'd memorize them in his head, then recite each line over and over until someone was able to sneak him in a pen, and he'd write them down on the back of cigarette paper.

Luba can hear the phone ring in the background but ignores it and instead turns to the first letter Roman had ever sent her. It's all about their first meeting, and now Luba only wants to remember; to breathe in the crisp air of that October evening and retrace the steps she'd forgotten she once took.

Appropriately enough, they'd met at a poetry reading. Roman, as master of ceremonies, had stood at the lectern and jingled some coins in his pocket, then looked across the room when Luba slipped into a seat at the back. He waited until she set her purse on the floor and settled back in the chair before starting the reading. At 42, Roman had a head full of curls and a smile so wide that even Luba, who was usually nervous around strangers, had been immediately set at ease. She knew all about Roman. She knew about his wife who'd been arrested along with him and later died of pneumonia in a Siberian labor camp. She knew about his only son who was raised by his maternal grandparents and had only seen his father a handful of times during his entire childhood. Later, Roman would tell her more about Oles and the letters Oles wrote documenting his day at school or a trip to the Black Sea with his grandparents. His letters were always precise and full of detail and never once mentioned the taunting he'd endured when one or another of his teachers would make note of his family background to the class.

When the poetry reading ended that night, Roman walked up to her at the *fourchette*, Luba's hand losing its grip on the wine glass she just lifted to her lips. He was quick, but not quick enough and caught her fingers as the glass slipped to the floor. They laughed about it later, shards of glass at their feet, fingers sticky from the red *Muscat* that splattered and spilled all over the white tablecloth and even on their clothes. Roman kissed Luba's hand then, bowing longer than necessary, and Luba could feel the warm touch of his lips settle on her skin with an almost easy familiarity. When she shivered, he rose immediately, releasing her hand from his grasp. They talked for the next two hours and continued their conversation while they walked downhill through the narrow, poplar-lined streets all the way to the Dnipro River. The metro had stopped running by then, and they stood at the river's edge. They talked and stared at one another, their flow of conversation finally cut short by some fishermen who arrived with the break of dawn. Roman hadn't kissed Luba again that night, but by the time he walked her to the door of her apartment building, Luba knew she was in love for the first time in her 36 years of life.

* * *

The knock on the door is soft at first and then turns loud, brazen almost in its intensity, distracting Luba from the stack of letters strewn across the bed.

"Not now," Luba says.

Marusia pokes her head in.

"It's Oles again. Luba, that's the fourth time he's called today," Marusia says. "He wants to go through Roman's papers. He needs some background information for the press."

"I don't want him poking around here. I haven't even had a chance to go through anything yet."

"Luba." Marusia's voice changes from determined to placating in the instant that it takes her to wipe her hands against her apron. "Come eat," she says. "I've made some *varenyky* for you. The sauerkraut ones that you like the best."

In spite of herself, Luba grins. Marusia hates cooking, and yet she's been steaming up the kitchen for the past three weeks, hoping all the fuss and banging of the pots and pans will bring Luba from her self-imposed solitude in the bedroom.

"You never cook *varenyky*," Luba says. "You're always complaining about how much work it is to make the dough, let alone fill and cook them afterward."

Marusia shrugs. "I know you loved it when he cooked them for you," she says.

Luba glances at her sister, whose face is flushed from the heat in the kitchen, gray hair loosely bunched over the top of her head, hands clenched at her sides, as if expecting resistance and steeling herself for the next battle. The sight of Marusia's hands balled into fists drains all the warmth from Luba's voice.

"Can't you see I'm not ready to eat yet?" Luba asks. Her tone is even sharper than she intended, but before Luba can smooth it over, Marusia has stepped back out into the hall, head averted from Luba's gaze.

"Dinner in one hour, Luba," she says. "You can't relive the past forever."

The door clicks shut, and then Luba hears her sister's slippered footsteps moving down the hallway toward the front of the house. She should have kept her mouth shut, Luba thinks, but all she saw while Marusia spoke was Roman standing in the kitchen, his sleeves rolled up to the elbows, Luba's old apron hanging loosely to his knees.

Luba always expected she'd be the one to go first since Roman was so determined to hang on to life. He told her that he'd been the smallest child in the village who was lucky enough to live through the *Holodomor*—the great famine that Stalin created to force the peasants into collectivizing their land. Luba's own life was quite ordinary in contrast, until she'd turned eight, and the war started. After her father was killed and the Nazis had come and gone, and the communists had settled in for good, Luba's mother fussed over her younger daughter so much that Luba escaped her hometown as soon as possible. Those were the years that Luba herself came under close watch, when she met with friends in cafes and hideaways, when printing clandestine pamphlets and forbidden literature filled her with as much energy and joy as her childhood friends found in raising children.

Maybe it was because she never had her own children that Luba wanted to become close to her stepson. She envisioned cooking scores of meals for Oles and baking golden-brown *medivnyk* or her favorite poppy seed torte. After she married Roman, Oles had been studiously polite and welcomed her into the family with a kiss on the cheek and a pat on the back. When she'd reached forward to hug him, Oles stepped back, almost stumbling in his surprise.

"He keeps his emotions in check," Roman always told her. "Except when he's arguing with me."

In fact, Oles was careful not to fight with his father in Luba's presence. Instead he'd shake his head and reach for his coat if a conversation took an unexpected turn, and Luba would walk him to the door, dutifully leaning forward as Oles kissed her good-bye on the cheek.

* * *

Luba's hour until dinnertime is almost up when the doorbell rings and she hears Marusia shuffling to the front of the house.

Oles' voice resonates through the rooms, and Luba moves closer to the door, trying to catch snatches of conversation. Oles is furious. Luba can hear it through the wall by the way his shoes creak over the hardwood floors, back and forth, up and down, from one end of the house to another. Oles hasn't bothered to take off his shoes at the door, and without warning, indignation pushes Luba out of her bedroom.

Oles is surprised by Luba's appearance. Luba can tell that he's taken aback by the way he nervously clears his throat, scans her from head to toe, shifts his weight from one foot to another. Luba can see that the fact that she's barely eaten in weeks and only ran a hurried hand through her hair doesn't escape his attention. Oles is used to seeing Luba at her best, hair coiffed and nicely dressed with a touch of face powder disguising her pale complexion. Oles eyes her in silence, and Luba bristles.

"What do you need from me?"

"You can't hide in here forever."

They both speak at once and then pause and then try once again.

"I need time to grieve," Luba begins.

"Your voice needs to be heard now too," Oles says.

The door to the kitchen slips shut, and then Marusia turns on the water faucet, letting Luba know she must clear the air with her stepson.

"Let me be blunt. Whatever you may think, I wasn't happy about your disagreements with your father," Luba says.

Oles nods. "I told him this political campaign was a mistake," he says. "He only laughed and said I was acting like an old man scared of his own shadow. Now he's in the ground, and the investigation's ready to rule it was an accident."

"He couldn't accept your fear," Luba murmurs.

"I'm talking about common sense," Oles says.

"You're talking as though people can change who they are," Luba says. "You knew him better than anyone."

"Some days I'd just want to walk away from it all—from his poetry, from his past. I never had the guts to tell him that. But right now I feel the way I did when I was 10 years old, and all I wanted was to hear my father's voice," Oles says, and they look at each other from opposite ends of the room, waiting for a sign, a glimmer that all has not been lost, that the future without the man they both love holds more than discontent and despair.

It's Luba who finally breaks the silence. "He always liked it when you stood up to him," she says. "Even when he didn't agree with you. 'That's my boy. That's the spirit. That's something he got from me,' he'd say."

"That sounds just like him," Oles says, and without warning he crosses the room until he's standing right next to Luba. She hears him swallow several times, as if he's tasting the words before he can release them. "You look bad," Oles says, patting her hand as though she's a child. "He wouldn't have liked it. He wouldn't have liked it one bit."

Luba stands there, so surprised that she can't say anything. She can only stare at the corners of the room as if the answer to all her troubles could be found in the strokes of paint that cover the blemishes in the wall that Roman had filled in after they'd first moved in. The painters had missed some spots, and Roman had insisted on doing the work himself. He had spent most of the day crouched on the ladder like an artist, laying on brushstroke after brushstroke, as if he was painting a religious icon, a masterpiece to be unveiled before an unsuspecting crowd. For the first time since his death, just as Oles lets go of her hand and steps away, Luba senses Roman's presence as though he's standing right next to her. That feeling only lasts a few seconds, but it's enough to make Luba smile.

* * *

Forty days after Roman's death, when it is believed that the soul ultimately departs the earth, Luba heads to the cemetery carrying a basket filled with wine, *varenyky* and a small photo album filled with pictures of Luba and Roman's trip to Crimea from the previous summer. Oles is meeting her at the grave site, and together they will sit on a blanket, drink wine and discuss the man who left them behind. Although they've only spoken a few times on the telephone, with each conversation Luba finds that they talk for a few minutes longer, and she no longer dreads her stepson's calls. Since Marusia's gone back to her home in Western Ukraine, Luba's taken to talking on the phone more than she'd expected, and she called for an independent inquiry into Roman's death. Tomorrow she'll hold her first press conference. But today, she hopes that she and Oles will discuss more than the recent past, that he'll have photos of his own to share, that he'll talk about his wife Olena and son Marko, and better yet, invite Luba to a school play or a casual dinner. She'd love to see her grandson on stage and tell him stories about his grandfather, stories that Roman passed on to her. She hopes that Marko will one day pass on those same stories to his own grandchildren and understand why Luba believes that Roman won't be forgotten, that one day their country will become everything Roman had dreamed of.

Luba knows that's hoping for a lot. When she gets to the cemetery, Oles is already there, head cocked to the sky. It's a cool day, and the sun is half-hidden by clouds, but Luba can hear the birds singing around them as if life is just beginning, and one has only to reach deep inside to let the melody take hold.

23

The Artist

It was the type of thing he normally had no patience for, but Nadia had been so insistent over the phone. She wanted him to go to some new exhibit they'd just put on with artifacts practically scooped up fresh from the excavation site and carried away for display to the Pechersk Museum. "By-zan-tine," she'd purred, drawing out the syllables for emphasis. And Valeriy could imagine her broad smile, her fingers twisting the phone cord in a spiral, as if that word alone would be enough to get his ready assent.

His passion for anything remotely connected to the medieval past was as familiar to Nadia as his kisses had once been, but Valeriy still held back in answering, hesitating to commit so readily.

"You know you want to come," Nadia said. "So why play coy with me? Who knows, it might even get you to pull out the paint brushes."

"Don't count on it," Valeriy said, although he'd actually meant to say don't count on me, but by then Nadia had already hung up, laughing in lieu of saying goodbye.

His passion for Byzantine art aside, Nadia knew precisely how he felt about the current gallery scene and the art openings that had sprung up all over Kyiv in the last few years: champagne glasses and a room full of forced smiles while everyone gaped at canvases bursting with bizarre slabs of color. Each brushstroke resembled a frenzied glob of paint, and there was no sense of cohesion. At least, that was the type of art they were showing down at the fancy galleries, charging hundreds of dollars in the hope that some foreigner or one of those mafia-connected businessmen running free in the country would loosen their wallets.

Valeriy kept far away from that scene, hardly bearing the thought that these days, success as an artist was being measured by the appearance of one's work in those very same galleries. He didn't want his paintings ending up in the hands of some so-called New Ukrainian, slicked-back hair and cell phone in hand, who discussed suspect dealings over the phone as casually as other people discussed their dinner plans.

Instead, Valeriy felt more comfortable about entrusting his paintings to people like his Babtsia, who hadn't gotten her pension for the last seven months and spent every Sunday down at the local bazar, selling vegetables from her garden for a few extra *kopiykas*. He'd wanted her to sell the paintings when the pension money stopped coming in, but she refused to sell any of the ones she had and hung them over the entire house so that scenes of Kyiv's golden-domed churches were displayed next to an array of historical portraits.

"Things aren't quite so bad that I have to sell my only grandson's artwork," she said. "Besides I'm saving these for your exhibition. They'll be hanging right alongside your new work."

But Valeriy wasn't doing much painting these days. At least since he'd come back from being in the United States for an entire year on a cultural exchange. He'd returned to Ukraine with eyes gaping, not at the memory of Chicago with its 24-hour lighted aisle ways filled with everything from deodorant spray to plastic Ziploc bags, but at his own country, which had finally gotten to call itself independent but was now in worse shape than before he'd left. When he'd arrived in Kyiv, he'd walked around like a daft old man who'd fallen out of a moving car, for three whole months elbowing away the shoves that greeted him every time he'd stepped into the metro or had to fight his way through the open sliver between bodies onto the tram. The eyes were what he couldn't thrust away, no matter how hard he butted his shoulders in through the subway door during his first few weeks back in Ukraine, until he'd finally realized no one was going to step aside or smile the way they did back in Chicago. The eyes here were more bleak and hard than before he'd left, or maybe he'd grown soft in the 12 months he'd been away. Maybe he'd also begun smiling in the way they did over there. He'd been back home for a year now, but he still hadn't picked up a paintbrush, or rather picked it up only to throw it back down again, the urge to paint gone as quickly as it had come.

* * *

Even though Nadia had laughed on the phone, Valeriy knew she was counting on him to show up this time, thinking that drawing him into the circle of his former art acquaintances was one step away from getting him to paint. His art was the one thing the two of them had never argued about, and it was Nadia, more often than not, who modeled for his series of historical portraits.

"Just think," she'd said time and again. "Someday you can show your work exclusively in my gallery, and we'll use the extra earnings to buy our own *dacha.*"

Even then, she was thinking ahead to the future, picturing herself as the successful businesswoman, Valeriy the popular artist, their lives linked as surely as honeybees clustered on a spray of nectar. When Valeriy had received the news he'd been chosen to go abroad, Nadia had been more excited than him. She had thrown her arms around his neck and wrestled him to the ground, squealing like a child. It was only later that night after they'd made love and were sitting outside on the balcony in the dark smoking cigarettes, that Valeriy told her he'd be gone for a year. Nadia had turned to him with an abrupt motion of her head.

"You are coming back, aren't you Valeriy?" she asked.

At the time, he'd been surprised by the urgency in her voice. He'd never really considered living anywhere else, but with the question thrown so unexpectedly in his face, Valeriy hesitated. After a minute, Nadia had gotten up and gone inside, and even though Valeriy knew he should have gone in after her, he'd sat alone in the dark, smoking down the rest of the pack.

* * *

They were all waiting for him inside the exhibit hall as if it was his work gracing the walls instead of Byzantine relics. Nadia had her hair up, the anxious look in her eye reminding Valeriy of a woebegone child. She probably thought he wouldn't show up like he hadn't the last time she'd invited him to an opening at the art gallery where she worked as a manager. On that night, Valeriy had put on his only good suit with that tie of ridiculous yellow smiley faces that he'd picked up on the sale rack in a Chicago mall. He'd returned from the States a couple of months earlier, and although initially he'd been glad to be back home, Valeriy found that his year away from Ukraine had left behind an indelible mark. He no longer wanted to smoke. He no longer wanted to drink all night, sitting around the table with his university friends, sliding down shots of vodka like water slipping down a parched throat. He no longer wanted to face endless questions about why he left or came back home for that matter. But the most frightening aspect of it all was that Valeriy no longer wanted to paint. The historical portraits he'd been so driven to portray now seemed as insignificant as the Soviet rubles that'd been replaced by the new Ukrainian currency. Even the landscapes no longer beckoned, and Valeriy had realized this as he stood outside the gallery, then finally spit on the sidewalk in disgust and walked away.

That was last time. Tonight, Nadia was all smiles now that Valeriy stood before her.

"So nice of you to show up," she said teasingly, twisting her arm around his as if this easy banter had existed between them all along; as if Nadia hadn't cried at the airport when Valeriy left for the States; as if Valeriy hadn't almost turned back at the last minute, almost willing to forego the opportunity of a lifetime. He'd only called her once from Chicago, after he'd kissed another girl, and she'd guessed from the sound of his voice that something was amiss, but Valeriy had lied and told her nothing had changed.

"Nadia claimed this would get you out of your hole." Red-faced Oleh, gripping Valeriy's hand, pressed his lips up against Valeriy's ear, his breath stinging with liquor. "When will you bring me some of your scenic landscapes? The tourists are always clamoring for those."

And then voices were coming at him from all sides.

"Valeriy, it's been so damn long. We all thought you'd gone back to America, the way you've slipped, simply vanished from the scene."

"Hey, old man, it's good to see you back. Someone said you lived in Canada now."

The faces were familiar, and for a moment Valeriy breathed in the convivial air of camaraderie pressing him nearer to the circle, the perspiring handshakes and wet kisses, even Nadia's uneven sighs as welcoming as the cognac he had downed to jumpstart his flagging spirits when the painting had first stopped.

Somebody gripped his shoulder, and Valeriy winced, peering up at Tanya Hrytsenko's pudgy face, her smile broad and a bit crooked. "Where have you been hiding, you stupid fool?" Her voice in his ear was insistent, petulant even. "Took off for the States without so much as a goodbye, and don't think I've forgotten about that hundred you still owe me."

"Tetianka." For a second, Valeriy was happy to see her and embraced the chubby woman.

Tanya twisted in his arms. "You've changed. Gotten thinner. No, that's not it. It's your eyes. You look forlorn, like a lost kid or something," she said as she

30

pushed his head back and scrutinized him with the serious air of a doctor.

Valeriy stepped back, grinning at her concern. "You've gotten stout, old woman," he said, tapping her chin. "And you never were one to keep your thoughts to yourself, even when no one's asking for your advice."

"Aah, Valeriy." For a minute Tanya looked affronted before letting out a laugh. "You're still not mad at me, are you? You got to go to America in the end. I didn't tell that director you shouldn't go, just with all the privileges you had, there might be other artists he could have picked."

"You're not bringing that up?" Nadia asked, stepping between the two of them, surveying first Tanya and then Valeriy. "You never know when to keep quiet, Tanya, even after all this time."

"I never said a bad word about his paintings, did I? Even though it's a damn shame he's translating articles for some business weekly instead of taking advantage of that talent of his."

They were talking about him as if he were on the other side of the room, if not on the other side of the ocean, and Valeriy suddenly had no desire to hear any more of the conversation. It almost seemed as if they were talking about a stranger. Truthfully, Valeriy felt decades rather than only six years removed from the student he'd been when he went against his father's wishes and demonstrated against the Soviet government, even hunger striking with the others.

"Don't you even care that I'm standing right here?" He'd only meant to mutter the words aloud, but once they managed to slide from his lips and hurtle through the restraint he usually imposed on himself, Valeriy found himself yelling, his voice slicing through the din.

"Just like always." After a moment, Tanya wagged her head. "Never know what's inside that boy. Didn't I warn you Nadia?" she asked.

But Valeriy was already striding into the other room, cursing them as much as himself. He'd come to look at the Byzantine exhibit, and frazzled or not, he'd allow himself the luxury to slip into a past where he could observe to his heart's content and not have to worry about giving anything of himself in return.

* * *

"Long before you were born, long before even your grandmother's grandmother was born, Kyiv was the capital of a great empire. But like many great empires, after a long period of prosperity and wealth, greed overtook

wisdom, and brother turned against brother, weakening that which was once insurmountable."

When Valeriy was a boy, his father would recite these words to him at the start of their history lesson, which took place every Sunday afternoon around the square table in their kitchen, his father seated at one end like a commander-in-chief, and Valeriy, the cowering soldier, directly across from him at the opposite end. And even though Valeriy came to dread these lessons, fearing rebuke from his father for a wrong answer or even a carelessly worded one, he found that his interest in this medieval era all began at that kitchen table. That was where his father spoke of royal rulers who loved a good battle and cities filled with Byzantine palaces and gold-studded churches that dazzled visitors with their cascades of frescoes and mosaics. The mosaics were always his favorite: color and stone fusing into a vivid image that mesmerized Valeriy, made him marvel at the painstaking precision of the process, as well as the result.

It was a mosaic that stopped him now too. Volodymyr, the ruler of Kyiv-Rus', was staring at him with a somber, almost sorrowful gaze. He'd converted his country to Christianity by forcing all the residents to step into the great river that flowed through the city while the priests performed the rite of baptism. Coldness. Ice. Power. That was what Valeriy expected to find in the eyes of this leader. But instead, Valeriy saw a touch of sadness, as if he knew what would befall his country in the following centuries. Or maybe it was only what Valeriy wanted to see; the same way he'd wanted to see a softening on his father's face when he looked at Valeriy's paintings.

"You know for all the power he wielded, his own wife despised him," Nadia's voice startled Valeriy, and he shrugged, moving away from the wall.

"What's it got to do with me?" he asked.

"What's anything ever got to do with you, Valeriy?" Nadia sighed, her exasperation evident. "We haven't seen each other in months. I thought this exhibit could . . ."

"Not down that road again," Valeriy cut in as his fingers lifted to touch Nadia's arm, then brushed against her skin.

"Maybe you're assuming too much. Think about that." Nadia's response was quick, her lips curling as she shifted her arm but didn't move it away. "I just thought you might get inspired being here around these relics you seem to love so much," she said.

Valeriy grinned, moving his hand away. "You don't really believe it's all over, do you?" he asked.

But Nadia shook her head, not even paying attention to his words. "You can't do it, can you?" she asked. "You've really given up?"

"Hold on." Valeriy moved forward, unable to turn away from the matter-of-factness in her question. "Hold on now. I was talking about us," he said.

"I was talking about you," she said.

* * *

They'd met in the fall of 1990 when changes were sweeping their country at a pace that no one could have foretold. "Sovereignty" and "breaking away" became words no longer lodged in one's throat like butterflies struggling to free themselves from the collector's net. Students set up their tents and unrolled their sleeping bags on the square under the statue of Lenin and began demanding changes from the government. The ones that were hunger striking wore white bandannas tied around their heads, and that was how Valeriy first spotted Nadia, cropped hair and freckles splashed across her face. Her eyes sparkled with an enthusiasm that made Valeriy set aside his own uncertainty.

"They're saying the girls shouldn't be allowed to hunger strike," were her first words when he'd walked over to introduce himself. "They tried to talk us out of participating. But we all came anyway."

Valeriy had worn the white bandanna himself, one of about 200 students who'd turned the square in downtown Kyiv into a campsite brimming with local and foreign journalists, politicians and residents amazed at what happened in their very midst. When two weeks passed, and the prime minister resigned, Valeriy felt buoyed by a power as fierce as when he'd first splayed paint over a canvas with his brush, colors springing to life while he worked feverishly, minutes and hours meshed into one; the wind at his back like a blade, back and forth, no time to stop, no time to breathe, no time to lose the momentum of the dance—Valeriy had simply painted as if his life were at stake.

It was like that after the hunger strike too. Change. It had seemed so simple, Valeriy thought. Make a few demands, obtain some promises, and it appears as though the entire landscape around you can alter. Trees felled, roads opened and paved, even foreign slogans sprung up on billboards that overlooked streets once trapped in the past.

They'd all felt so energized then, as if all the hours in the day and night weren't enough to soak up the manic momentum brought on by the breakup of the Soviet empire. Nadia talked of free elections, Western fashions and business ventures while Valeriy read previously banned history books and painted, one historical portrait after another. Nadia posed in medieval clothes for him by day and the two of them fell together into bed at night.

When they'd gotten around to talk about their families, Valeriy had described his father as a stubborn old man, and then he added that his convictions were red, as beet red as the *borsch* Nadia cooked for them when the weather turned cold. The chauffeur and the car, the backyard with the fountain spouting water through the open snout of a dolphin, even the annual vacation packages to the top Crimean and Carpathian hideaways—for years Valeriy had taken it all for granted. When he'd entered the university in Kyiv, far from the city in northwest Ukraine where he'd grown up, Valeriy found it easy to let go of the past. Almost as if by wiping the slate clean, he could undo all the knots that bound him, like a faithful dog, to the family homestead.

* * *

When Valeriy first arrived in Chicago, he'd written to Nadia almost every single week and told her in letters the words he'd been unable to express in person.

"I'm not staying here forever," Valeriy had written on the side of an envelope. "Never doubt I'll come back," he'd penned on the back of a postcard of the Buckingham Fountain. Every Friday Valeriy headed to the main post office downtown and sent each letter by registered mail, not wanting to risk the machinations of the Ukrainian postal system.

Bustling with people and outdoor activities, Chicago had reminded him of Kyiv. During the warmer months, Valeriy had taken the bus from the Ukrainian Village neighborhood where he lived and taught classes in painting, to Lake Michigan, easel in hand. He loved to feel the wind on his face, and Valeriy would sit there for hours on end, sometimes painting, sometimes only to watch the color of the skyline and the children play along the shoreline, recalling his hometown until the sounds of English reinforced the fact that he was in a foreign land. At first he believed it would be difficult to paint in an unfamiliar setting, but in spite of himself, the peaceful monotony of day to day allowed him to explore new techniques, experiment with light and shadow and for a little while at least, Valeriy could relax and convince himself that he'd lived in America all along.

The local Ukrainians in the area, the ones who'd lived there for decades and were more American than Ukrainian in some ways and more Ukrainian than American in others, had taken him in. In the beginning, he'd been impressed at how they'd all preserved the language and passed it down to their children and grandchildren like a cherished book. They'd built schools and credit unions, sent their kids to scout and dance camps and knew more about Ukrainian history and the works of political dissidents than many of Valeriy's closest friends. But after a while, Valeriy found that their inclination to dish out political advice grated on him.

"They should just lock up all those communists," Pani Olya, Valeriy's landlady, told him every single day. "Look at Poland. They outlawed the Communist Party. They don't want to live in the past."

Others tried to talk him into staying and building a new life for himself in the relative comfort of a stable economy. And Valeriy couldn't argue that opportunities here were tangible and assured in a way that would be a long time coming back home. But he still dreamed of going back, even after his letters to Nadia slowed and, for a time, stopped altogether. It wasn't about kissing another woman or remembering Nadia's eyes at the airport. It wasn't even the fact that Nadia didn't respond to half of his letters, and when she did, wrote effusively about new friends and shops setting up business in the city. He missed the old-world history that was tucked inside the slopes overlooking the *Dnipro* River or branded onto pieces of surviving medieval architecture that no Chicago skyscraper could ever replace. He also missed dropping in on friends unannounced at all hours of the day and night, although he knew that if he stayed in America long enough, even this would be replaced by something new. At the age of 26, Valeriy was afraid to start his life all over again, but what he didn't expect when he finally made it back home to Kyiv was that this was precisely what he'd end up doing anyway.

* * *

The Byzantine exhibit was still going strong at the museum, but Valeriy edged toward the door in need of fresh air. He spotted Nadia in the midst of a group as she hoisted a glass of red wine to her lips. He considered waving or even walking up but found himself on the street unable to determine which strategy seemed best. He decided to walk as if movement would focus his mind on something other than the past he'd just left behind at the museum.

One block turned into two, then 10 and 20, and soon any trace of time and memory became lost as Valeriy roamed through Kyiv, his fingers tracing the outlines of looming church domes, rounded archways and spires, feet slowing at every sharp incline, up steps and narrow, chipped sidewalks; past statues and poplar-enclosed boulevards, as if he'd be catching a plane out on the following morning and would never be coming back. The old *babusias* were still out by the *Zoloti Vorota* metro stop and showed no signs of packing up, *Sovietske champagnske* and *Svitoch* and *Korona* chocolate bars strewn about like offerings on a makeshift altar.

Valeriy slowed near them and thought about giving in to the sudden urge for a pack of cigarettes. He hadn't smoked in months, but now nothing seemed as right as heading across the alleyway and through the small park to stand at the foot of the Golden Gates to offer up plumes of smoke instead of the gold coins travelers had to pay to enter the city back in medieval times. All his roaming over the last couple of hours, which had taken him away from Nadia and a museum filled with Byzantine relics, now directly led him to what had been the main entrance into 11th-century Kyiv. Some of it was still intact. The original walls were preserved like a prehistoric fossil within the gateway church and adjacent ramparts that had been built to replicate the original. No one had ever been able to penetrate the Gates, not even the Mongols who'd spent 10 weeks battering the walls until they'd finally broken through another gate into the city.

Valeriy thought about touching the natural stone and yellow and red bricks that'd gone into the making of the arched walls. He imagined the deep moat spanned by a drawbridge that'd been ceremoniously lowered when a French king had sent his envoys to ask for the hand of one of King Yaroslav's daughters. He couldn't touch the original stone, but as he stood there smoking one cigarette after another, Valeriy could almost feel it in his palm; the cold touch of ancient stone that inexplicably proved soothing, not unlike a balm against an open wound.

* * *

After all his roaming, heading back home seemed like the obvious choice, but Valeriy found himself standing on the corner half a block away from the Pechersk Museum while he waited for Nadia. She finally emerged and would have walked straight past without a word if he hadn't caught her elbow.

"It was good you invited me, you know," he said. "It kind of gave me a perspective again."

"I can't remember the last time you thanked me for anything," she said, glancing at him suspiciously. "You're not broke, are you?"

"When did you become such a cynic?" Valeriy asked, laughing. "A few hours ago you were defending me to Tanya, and now you think I'm hitting you up for money."

Nadia shrugged. "We've all got our weak spots," she said.

They started walking then, around the corner and down the winding street in the direction of the metro. "How's your Babtsia?" she asked, after they walked for two blocks in silence.

"She's hanging in. 71 years old with a garden and an orchard to look after and she helps out the neighbors when she can," Valeriy replied. "My old man's still griping, but even he's talking about going into some kind of business and thinks I should get involved."

"At least you're speaking to each other now," Nadia said as they crossed down into the pedestrian walkway. In this part of the city, the passageway was dark, and Valeriy gripped Nadia's hand, moving her from the path of a drunken man staggering forward. Another old woman sat on the steps with a cup of coins in her lap.

"Yeah, at least we're talking now. That's a start," he said as they walked into the metro station.

He thought about telling her that his father had looked at him as though he was crazed when Valeriy had showed up on his doorstep after 12 months of being away. "Can't you ever do anything right in your life? Don't you see that everything around you is falling apart?" his father had asked before shaking his head and turning away.

Valeriy thought about telling Nadia he'd wanted to call her so many times from Chicago, but the truth of the matter was he'd been afraid to hear her voice, or maybe he'd just been too afraid to admit how lonely he'd been. Maybe that's how he ended up being with another girl, who conveniently happened to be his landlady's niece, on one Chicago summer night. Valeriy wanted to talk and talk. All of a sudden he wanted Nadia to experience the relative ease he'd felt when he'd had no worries about money drying up for groceries or a box of paints. He'd never told her about Chicago, not really, about what it was like to be displaced in not just one culture but two. But at the last second, Valeriy simply gripped Nadia's hand tighter then ran his finger against her palm.

"What's on your mind, Valeriy?"

Valeriy spun to a stop, turning Nadia round to face him. "Why'd you really invite me tonight?" he asked.

"Why'd you really stop painting?" she asked.

"Oh, come on, Nadia. If this is a game of questions, I've got a stack full for you too. You barely responded to my letters."

"What did you want me to say?" Nadia asked. "We made no promises. You only said you were coming back after you were already gone. And you never said you were coming back to me. Now you've been walking around for months like a man who's lost his soul." Nadia paused before continuing. "Maybe it's not like we dreamed it, but this is how our lives are now. This is how Ukraine is now."

"How do you do it, Nadia?" Valeriy asked. "It seems so easy for you. You never let go of your dreams."

"Maybe it's not as bad as you think," she said. "If you're real lucky, you find someone to grab on to, and then you just keep on going."

Valeriy didn't respond as he walked Nadia over to her side of the platform inside the station.

"Tanya was right, you know," he finally said. "Half the time I don't know what's inside of me. Back when we first met, it was mostly about pissing my old man off."

"Maybe it only started out like that," Nadia said.

The metro train pulled up then, and Nadia leaned close and kissed Valeriy on the cheek. "Call me when you start painting again," she whispered.

Valeriy watched as Nadia sprang into the car, squeezing her way through the aisle way without looking back. He stood as if rooted until the next incoming train ground to a halt, and people flew out in a swarm, jostling him with their bodies, pushing him along in their wake, unresisting, his body slack until they reached the edge of the staircase that led up to the exit. Valeriy moved to the side, his eye caught by an older couple who, oblivious to the crowd, spun to the beat of a street musician's accordion. They twirled around each other and laughed as hard as if they'd just won the lottery; as if happiness were at hand in this very place, this instant, in the very touch of their hands and the rhythm of their steps. Valeriy began clapping, first slowly and then more vigorously, harder and harder until his palms reddened, stung from the force.

"Perfect," he muttered under his breath, staring at the bright colors of clothing and swirling feet as if admiring a piece of art. "Simply perfect."

Whitewashed Sojourn

Sitting here, hunched on the back of the motorcycle behind Dimitri, I can feel the wind pressing the bike forward so steadily that we're gliding around the curves of the road like there are sails guiding the turns. And before I know it, I'm laughing so hard I can hardly breathe.

I haven't felt this fearless since that super-slide ride when I was 10. Babtsia stood waiting at the bottom while I slid my feet into the canvas sack and flew down, bump over bump, laughing and feeling like nothing, absolutely nothing, could get in my way. It's strange how I had to come all the way to Greece to recapture that feeling.

Maybe it's got something to do with being in a country where the sun's as friendly as the people, warming even the white buildings so they sparkle like marble pillars all across the island. It's been hard to feel downcast surrounded by the Greek light. Those moments usually pass quickly enough and I breathe a sigh of relief. I don't want to think much about how Mama's doing back home in Michigan or how I left my brother Danylo behind without a word of goodbye. I flew away with a green backpack stowed in the luggage compartment, dark sunglasses clamped over my eyes, a copy of Kazantzakis' *Zorba* gripped in my hand. I promised myself I'd get to know Greece like the locals did, even though my blue eyes and blonde hair give away that there's not a drop of Greek blood in me. But then I can't even tell you why I picked Greece for my destination in the first place. I left Detroit in the middle of a school semester when the snow and slush hadn't completely melted away, dropped all my classes like I was going through a shopping list, then stopped at the student ticket office on the way home. Getting away seemed so simple that when I spotted the poster of whitewashed homes zig-zagged against the sharp drop of a cliff, an azure-blue sky in the background, I only pointed at the poster and smiled at the ticket agent.

"Hey Sophika." Here in the open air, against the pull of the wind, Dimitri's voice is choppy and loud and tumbles over the din of the motor. Not only has he taken to calling me by the Ukrainian version of my name, he's picked up my manner of speaking, the way I like to talk in short, crisp sentences to reveal just the right amount of information and not a fraction more.

"Look," he says. "Nice view. I'll take some pictures."

When I don't respond, Dimitri darts his dark head back toward me with one hand and motions at the road which dips to the right. The twists ahead remind me of a roller coaster—bends stretch from side to side with only secluded spots of ground and foliage dangling over the edges of the precipice. Before I can answer, his eyes graze me with a hard look that contradicts the casual throw of his words.

"Okay," I say, my arms tight around his waist. "Just keep your eyes on the road, will you."

The bike jumps forward and Dimitri grins now, emits a low whistle through his teeth. Shaking my head, I stiffen and let my hands loosen so they're barely hanging on to his waist, but I don't let go. *Pictures*, I think. As if that's what it's about. I'm the one using my camera like a shield. I've taken pictures since I got here, and now Dimitri's caught up in it. He wants to jump behind the camera instead of in front of it and wants me to be in the spotlight, in focus, close-up—pale face, skinny legs and long hair which I plait in one thick braid down my back—he wants all of it in the frame of the lens. I figured he'd give up by now, wouldn't keep grilling me on my family and how I hardly write them, only mailing a few postcards in all these months. But I hope Mama understands, even if Danylo, who's 14, doesn't. Mama did the same when she was 20, only in her case it was an escape into a marriage that never worked. It didn't even have to be that last fight when she found those grade transcripts in my desk drawer. After Babtsia died, Mama and I couldn't stand to be close to each other. No sooner in the door than I'd want to turn around again before the circle of recriminations would begin. Maybe if she'd always been that way I would have taken it better, but it was as if Mama just discovered she had kids after years of letting Babtsia fill that role. Leaving wasn't about school. Or about Babtsia. It was about a little bit of both. I'd never been unpredictable in my life, but now the only way out of the corner I found myself backed into was to fly away from everything familiar as quickly as possible.

Dimitri hasn't dropped any of it though, the sidelong glances at the postcards lying face-up on the dresser. "Saving these for someone?" he asks, his voice completely matter-of-fact. It's absurd the way he picks up the cards in his hand and holds them, studies them like he's looking for the key to a puzzle. They're mostly blank though, just a few smeared lines of indistinguishable print tossed aside like a whim when I realized Mama didn't even like the sea. She couldn't get over the horrific tossing of the ocean liner that'd brought her over to America when she was 12 years old and trembling at the unknown. When I don't answer, Dimitri gets that knowing look in his eye, drops the cards from his fingers and bites his lip. He starts talking about something else, but he holds on to that look. Dimitri's so bright-eyed, but he can't see I'm still muddling through the paces of my life like the awkward kid I was in high school, couldn't coordinate a dance step no matter how hard I'd practice, while he moves forward with a sure step, a restaurant, kids and a wife all mapped out in his head. A fist full of plans like they're candy, and all he has to do is swallow them down to make it all happen.

But that's Dimitri, all right. Always laughing and joking with the tourists even after hours on his feet. After he's run in so many circles from the kitchen to the tables, he knows that path better than his own bed. Dimitri's usually the last one out of the restaurant, long after the Greek owner's finished his cigar, done eyeballing the lithe, British girl bartending in the cafe next door and has walked away, leaving Dimitri to set the chairs upside down atop the tables. It's been four months since we met, but it almost feels like four years the way I can predict Dimitri's apologetic shrug when I show up at the café. All the other waiters are long gone while he still sweeps up the floor around the kitchen.

Dimitri slows down now, but I barely notice until the motorbike grinds to a halt.

"It's one of the best views on the island," Dimitri announces as he walks toward the edge of the embankment. A hillside of white buildings and barren ground sweeps away from the road, tottering hundreds of feet down to the water below.

"Why won't you go with me?" he asks, turning around, eyes probing.

I stare at Dimitri, who stands still like a statue, as though I'll speak so softly that he has to be motionless to hear the words.

"I don't know. I don't want to send the wrong message."

"The wrong message?" Dimitri shouts. "What are you talking about? If you don't want this, say it. Why don't you just say it?" he asks, brushing the thick hair back from his face.

"Look," I say and clench my fingers against my palm. "I'm just not sure about meeting all of them, with my mom and all. I came here to get away from that."

"It's not natural, you cutting yourself off like you do," he says. Dimitri's so close to his family that when he was in the States two summers ago, he sent weekly letters back to Greece. He doesn't understand that I need this distance from Mama as much as he needs me to meet his family, and so he shakes his head, drops his eyes and digs in his pocket to pull out and light a cigarette. He inhales deeply as I swallow and fight for words to answer him.

He looks up, dark eyes staring me down. "I've told them about you," he says.

His eyes, pleading almost, remind me of Danylo; of how my brother looks at me after I yell at him for wanting to tag along when I go out with my friends; the way he looked the last time we saw Babtsia alive, all shriveled up in the hospital with tubes sticking out from her like they were quills. It was hard to even lean over and touch her without fingering the plastic that kept her breathing. Danylo's eyes haunted me so much I went away so I wouldn't have to face him since I couldn't stand seeing that pained look like I was deserting him by leaving him alone with Mama, like I was a coward for running away from it all.

"Just for a long weekend. Enough time to see everyone and show you around the village. Meet the family." Dimitri speaks quickly, syllables tumbling so I have trouble comprehending his words.

And looking up at his face, his cheeks flushed with color, I find that I can only nod, my throat dry, while Dimitri swings me round in a tight embrace.

* * *

On our last night on the island, Dimitri leads me down the road—past all the flashing neon discos, Irish bars and cafe clubs blaring music through loudspeakers and filled wall to wall with tourists—and down to a small restaurant club. We sit at a circular table to sip wine and listen to a tape of slower-paced Greek music, almost like a folk melody. When the beat quickens, Dimitri pulls me to my feet and drags me behind him onto the dance floor.

I stiffen, trying to take my hand away. "You know I don't dance," I plead. "Not like this, anyway. I mean, I was always the big joke at those things."

"No more excuses. Not like the other times," Dimitri looks down at me. "Still afraid," he challenges me after a minute, letting my hand go. "Always scared of something, aren't you?"

I look away, take a deep breath then step forward and rest one arm on Dimitri's shoulder while he grasps my other hand and squeezes it hard. Before I can protest, we spin around the room, and all I can hear is the sound of *bouzouki* and the drone of voices coming at me from a distance as we spin erratically from one side of the room to another. It's as if the rhythm has gotten into my feet and won't let me falter or think, much less look down at the floor in fright. I can hear the laughter gurgle in my throat, but I can't let go and take the chance of throwing off the momentum of the steps. But then it's all too much for me and I laugh, an inexcusable chortle, Dimitri scanning my face in surprise.

"It's okay," I say, and then his hand presses even tighter against my back, and there's no slowing down, only a tight three-stepped spin being woven across the floor, and I can hardly feel my toes. It's all a whirl, like that ride in the amusement park, Dimitri's feet guiding the way, and the only thing I can do is hang on and follow as I feel my lips widen and imagine the giddy smile that's plastered across my face.

* * *

On the night we met, it seemed pure chance that I found myself drawn to the small cafe where Dimitri worked, especially since the *Plaka* Cafe's not on the paved road built alongside the beach like most of the other restaurants. That's the main stretch where tourists amble from storefront to storefront, into one restaurant for *tzatziki* and feta salad and then into another for *moussaka* and *dolmades*. The thing I like best about Greek dining is that it feels like a picnic as everyone sits under the stars with tables set up in courtyards in front of the restaurants so I get a chance to look at the food before I take a seat. Next to the restaurants, postcards and T-shirts line the outside racks of the storefronts down the thoroughfare. On mornings when I'm not working at Despina's dress shop, I like to stand there among the store racks and finger the postcards to drown my thoughts in the glossy blue and red hues of Aegean water and sunsets. I usually start out with 10 postcards in my hand before placing them back, one by one, in their fitted slots on the rack. I settle on one or two cards that I later carry back to my room to marvel once more at the glossy color of a whitewashed church or the slope of a black cat's back, sunning itself on a window ledge.

Most of the other restaurants were filled with diners when I arrived on the island. On my first night, I walked down the promenade past restaurant after restaurant of smiling, white-shirted waiters who beckoned me into their establishments like the carnival barkers I used to see down at the State Fair when I was a kid. All I wanted to do was run away from that mayhem.

And then I spotted the *Plaka* after rounding a corner into a square filled with more rows of restaurants and shops with waiters who scurried from tables to the kitchen down narrow pathways, trays filled and held shoulder-high so that it seemed impossible they wouldn't collide. The *Plaka* was hidden in the corner, a scattering of tables and chairs placed outside. American rock music blared from a tape recorder near the door. It was small enough so I didn't feel intimidated by being alone and feeling like everyone was watching me. It's inevitable, the people watching that goes on.

The Greek men sit there for hours on end with a cup of dark coffee at their elbow, eyes unwavering as they take in each and every passerby with precise detail. When they're not on the watch, as I call it, they sit around the table with cards in their hand as cigarette smoke curls around them. I never see any Greek women with the men at the table no matter how many times I pass by. The older women I see, all dressed in black, hunch on small stools near their doorsteps in silence, eyes bright and watchful. I wonder what they think of all these tourists wandering over their island, clattering down the streets with the familiarity of long-lost relatives.

So there I was, sitting at a corner table at the *Plaka* sipping *retsina*, when the entertainment got underway. After slipping in a tape of Greek music, all three of the *Plaka* waiters joined hands, circling in front of the cafe. Slow, deliberate steps, knees rising in unison, changed over into a quicker pace, with knees and feet flying so quickly that I couldn't tell where one step ended and the other began. Even Takis, the owner, came out and turned up the recorder so that the quick folk beat filled with the strains of *bouzouki* spilled into the streets. Takis, who is gray-haired and grizzled, yet surprisingly sharp-eyed when it comes to women, sat there with his fingers tapping against a glass of *ouzo*, nodding indulgently while the customers all laughed and clapped their hands. When it ended, Dimitri, the tallest of the waiters, came over with a wide grin on his face and offered his damp palm in greeting. "Sophia," he muttered when he heard my name. "A Greek name. It means

46

wisdom, you know," he said, grinning. Smiling halfheartedly, I took his hand even though I couldn't help thinking about how easily I got away from Michigan, barely taking the time to pack before boarding the next available flight.

* * *

Away from the Cycladic islands, from the bright buildings and clear metallic blue of the Aegean Sea, I feel as if I've entered another realm. Looking out the bus window on our way to Dimitri's hometown, I see that the countryside is covered in greenery with houses bearing their traditional coloring of brown, tan and gray, a sight that's interspersed here and there with strings that buckle under an array of fluttering clothes. White linens soar like kites let loose in the wind. Gradually the countryside turns more sparse so that when we reach the outskirts of Larsina, Dimitri's village, the paved road gives way to one of dirt and stones with wild flowers growing along the roadside. I feel as though I could be back in the States, on the back roads near Howell, Michigan, where I spent my childhood years at Ukrainian scout camp. Reluctant at first, I ended up loving those camps where I'd invariably pick wild flowers and weave them into small wreaths which I'd later disperse among the other girls in the camp. Wreaths were special, like a good luck charm, Babtsia often told me, all part of that old country folklore she brought with her from Ukraine. Floating candlelit wreaths set adrift in rivers on the midsummer Feast of *Kupalo* were not only supposed to bring good fortune but a husband, too. Babtsia was good at telling the stories, at wanting me to believe in their magic, even when Mama would shake her head and scold Babtsia for filling my head with utter nonsense. And after a while as I grew older, wreath-making lost its charm. The very last wreath I'd woven had been pressed into Babtsia's hand, its colorful bloom buried with her on a snowy January day.

Only now, I discover that even with the dirt road and all the flowers, it can't be Michigan after all, since this road is much too narrow and gives no admittance to two-way traffic. Buildings and coffee houses are set up close to the road and doors open as people fill the streets, greeting the bus with smiles and curious looks.

"See how the village comes out to welcome us," Dimitri jokes, then pushes open the window and sticks out his head.

"*Yasoo*, Bobys. Come by the house," he yells to a slender man on the street who runs up to the window and grips Dimitri's hand in a quick handshake. "*Argotera*," Dimitri shouts as the bus winds down the street. "I'll see you later."

Scrunched in my seat, I can't help but grin while people yell out the windows. They laugh and joke as if they're at a football game, and the home team just pulled into the parking lot.

* * *

It's been impossible not to feel like an outsider even as Dimitri's mother pats me on the shoulder and smiles at me nonstop all through dinner. I feel guilty for not understanding more Greek. His mother's a chubby woman with a broad smile and short gray hair who first looks me over with a sly smile and pats my hand once, twice and then a third time before she grabs me without warning and clasps me in a tight hug. For a moment I'm not sure how to respond. Mama has never had much use for hugs. At most, she'll give you a quick pat on the cheek when she wants to express some warmth. It was always Babtsia, with her blue eyes and coiled-up hair, who was generous with her kisses and hugs. She told me that after they came to a new country, a new home and a new language, Mama learned to keep everything inside, as if afraid that by letting it all go, she'd lose herself too.

Dimitri's mother holds no such restraints. She walks me into the dining room, arm in arm, then insists I sit at the head of the table. In my hesitant Greek, I offer to help, but Mrs. Lefidas waves away the offer so adamantly that I can't help feeling I've said the wrong thing. Plate after plate—soup, feta cheese, lamb and thick chunks of bread—are then passed my way until I finally protest. Dimitri's father, a stocky man who leaves most of the talking to his wife, rises and offers me a glass of red wine.

"From his own vat," Dimitri whispers into my ear. "Only for special occasions. So who do you think it's all for—me or you?" he asks, then like a little boy, pulls at a loose strand in my braid.

I lean away, warmth creeping over me as Mrs. Lefidas titters and winks at me from across the table.

And then the four of us raise our glasses. Four solid clinks, glass against glass, reverberate through the room. I look around the table at Mrs. Lefidas as she gestures for me to eat more, then at her husband who likes to whistle during dinner and finally at Dimitri. I suddenly feel less like a stranger and more like a friend who's dropped in for a visit.

That cozy spirit quickly dissipates when, as if by prearranged signal, relatives and friends arrive at the house, at first one by one, and then in twos and threes, all shouts and laughter. They eye me with such looks of curiosity that after the first hour I begin to look around the dining room in desperation, searching for a corner to hide in. I can see Dimitri hemmed in by some friends on the opposite side of the room, head thrown back in laughter, a burning cigarette in one hand and a shotglass of *Metaxa* in the other. Dimitri looks up and catches my eye over the succession of dark heads in the room. With a shift of his head, he urges me over, but I smile back and shake my head. It's Dimitri's first visit home after eight months of working on Fira, and I don't want to intrude on it.

Near me, round-faced aunts with the same dark eyes and smiles as Dimitri's mother push their children forward. All the while they chatter so quickly in Greek that I can hardly understand what they're saying. Uncle Petros, a balding man with thick eyebrows and a hoarse voice, waves his fingers around like a baton and gestures at me with the animation of a choir director. Another woman, her hair wrapped up in a bun, introduces herself as a neighbor, then grips my arm and pulls out several photos from her sweater pocket.

"*Toh yomoo*, my boy," she explains as she points at one of the photos where a clean-shaven man leans against a shiny blue car, eyes squinting against the sunlight, a baby clasped to his chest.

"Basil lives in Boston now with his wife and baby girl," she says and lifts up her chin in pride. "My only boy owns two restaurants. He wanted to leave, you know," she continues. "Good future, he said. How could I argue?" She sighs and raises her palms in the air, then half-turns and eyes me with a covert glance. "You and Dimitri move to America, too, after Greek wedding? Dimitri open nice restaurant like Basil."

I laugh. Not even Mama's that direct. Since Babtsia died, it's as if Mama wants to pry open every thought I've ever had, like she needs to get her hands on every wish that's been stored away. And when I'd refuse the plea in her voice, she'd say in a hard voice, "You always were a daydreamer. Just like him." As if daydreaming had hastened my father's stroke and left her alone with two kids, as though his stroke had killed something between them that hadn't already been dead a long time ago. I suck in my breath and forget the woman who's eying me, waiting for an answer.

"We haven't discussed that. I'm still—" I pause to search for the right word.

"Studying," I muster. "Back home, I left school in the middle of a semester. I just needed a break."

"With a good husband, a woman won't worry." She smiles at me. "And with babies, you'll be busy. I think Dimitri will marry you very soon."

I move away from her toward the door. Air is what I need. I fight my way through the crowd, head down and shift my shoulders to thrust through.

But when I reach the hallway, I find there's no easy escape as I encounter Dimitri who's crouched near a chair by an elderly woman.

"Sophika," His face breaks into a grin. "Meet my grandmother." He motions at the old woman, who simply stares, her hair loose around her shoulders.

"*Yasoo*," I nod and force a smile to my dry lips.

"*Yiayia*," Dimitri runs his hand over the old woman's head as though she's a child. "This is Sophia," I hear him tell her.

The woman turns her head toward Dimitri as her smile widens. The eyes that stared at me only a moment ago now soften and sparkle with such undisguised energy that I'm struck by the transformation.

She responds with a blur of Greek that I don't understand, but it doesn't matter because *Yiayia* turns to me, leans forward and clasps my hands within her own.

So soft, I think, yet her grip's strong and traps my fingers within her own. *Yiayia* nods and giggles at Dimitri. "She's special, eh Dimitri," she says. That much I understand as she exchanges a look with her grandson, and then I realize how Dimitri can keep nothing inside. His smile has already told his family more about our relationship than any words ever could.

I try to slip my fingers from *Yiayia's* grasp, afraid the old woman won't let go and at the same time fearful that she will. And then I can't help myself. Leaning forward, I press a kiss onto her cheek. Then wrestling my hand away, I hurry toward the front door. I hear Dimitri call after me just as I step outside.

I stand there on the doorstep and gulp in air like I've climbed up a precipice. The door opens and shuts abruptly. I fold my arms across my chest, not looking at him, not wanting to.

Dimitri steps forward with a cigarette in hand. "So say we take a walk now?" he asks, surprising me as he extends his other hand out until I give in and clutch his fingers to fall in step beside him.

* * *

This is a genuine Greek club, Dimitri assures me as we enter. No tourist operations in this part of the country, he says, no doubt remembering how much I complain about some of the clubs we've been to on the islands; the ones that play top American and British hits over and over in one nightclub after another.

Instead, I love hearing the Greek music, even though I don't understand most of the words. It's the folk melodies, especially, that draw me in. When I shut my eyes and listen, wind and trees whistle at me, and sometimes I even hear a quick gallop, like horses racing across a plain, and just for a second it seems like a beat from one of Babtsia's folk tapes. But when I open my eyes, I realize that the words are Greek and not Ukrainian, and Babtsia's folk tapes are far from my reach. It doesn't matter though. I still love the Greek music and the way it makes me feel all warm and soft inside, as if I can touch it, wrap it around my body like a cocoon, unknown words and all.

"So what's the big deal? Stay six more months, a year, whatever." His eyes are serious, not sparkling like the other times.

I lean back in my chair as my fingers toy with the glass of *retsina* Dimitri has brought over from the bar. "It's not so simple," I say, surprised to hear myself voice the words.

Dimitri hunches forward. "Very simple," he says. "Just stay."

I sip my wine and stare at his flushed cheeks, at the way his lips curl in frustration. "Maybe I'm thinking of going back. Even finishing school," I say.

"So go to school here if that's the problem."

"I just think it's time." I look up at Dimitri and want to reassure the worried look in his eye, brush the hair back from his forehead. Just for a second I think about how easy it would be to say yes and to put off thinking about school or making amends with Mama. How easy it would be to slip into Dimitri's arms and rest my face against his chest and pretend that everything would turn out right.

"So your mind's made up already?"

"Maybe you could visit me in the States, even stay for a while," I say.

"I've already been there, remember?" he says. "Two months was enough." He looks away and downs his drink.

"You didn't like the people?" I ask.

Dimitri shrugs. "People are people, good ones and bad ones like everywhere else. But Greece, it's my home, my roots," he pauses. "Maybe if

51

we're together though," he looks at me, a question in his eyes. "The next time it'd be different."

I hold his gaze, smile. "Yeah, maybe it would," I say, but my voice comes out raspy, my mouth unexpectedly and suddenly dry.

* * *

They call it the *zembekiko*. Dimitri told me about the dance one night when we were still on Santorini after-hours in a local club, and an old man walked over to the center of the floor and motioned for the two band members to play. He started out slowly, but I couldn't help being fascinated by the way his aged body took on a new life. His face, weathered from days in the sun, was somber, pained almost, as hands raised, he circled the floor while his feet marked an intricate pattern of steps. After a minute, Dimitri rose, then crouching down on one knee near the man, clapped lightly as the man continued dancing. The song ended but another one started up almost immediately, and this time it was Dimitri circling the floor, the old man clapping him on. I didn't realize how good a dancer Dimitri was until that night when his feet wouldn't stop, his hands fluid and alive, his face so lost in the music that I felt as if I was looking at a stranger rather than the man who held my hand moments earlier.

And here, tonight, it's happening all over again. The music playing loud, haunting, *bouzouki* swirling around us so that I can't stop my feet from tapping against the floor and Dimitri's up, making his way to the center of the room like it's been planned that way all along. Slow and easy, cheeks flushed, his hair flying, round and round, faster, and those flashing eyes.

Dimitri dances like he's a marked man with only moments to live, and I can see that for him, this is the way it's all meant to be, the way it should be and the only way it'll ever be. I can't picture myself 20 years from now, but I can see him, a slight paunch and maybe a slower step, but the energy in his body will be as animated as it is today, his feet circling the room, *bouzouki* all around, and the flashing eyes, those dark flashing eyes, gleaming—all of it, just like today.

Babtsia

L ina stood at the window, looking out at the wooden cupolas of St. Andrew's in the far distance, a loose smile across her lips, one hand pulling aside the curtain Babtsia had refused to let her wash. She was stubborn alright, that grandmother of hers. Yesterday Lina came back from the garden with tomatoes in her hand to find Babtsia at the sink, back hunched over the iron basin, a bar of brown soap clutched between her gnarled fingers.

"It's all right," Babtsia said, her oval face red under the blue kerchief she'd tied around her gray hair. Babtsia's nose rose haughtily when Lina tried to step beside her and help. "This is my work."

Her grandmother's back was arched and her tone affronted. "No, Linochka, don't interfere. These curtains require special care, extra attention. Now be a good girl," she nodded at Lina. "And sit down and talk to me. Tell me how your mama's doing. I can't wait until her visit in October."

Lina gave up and sat down as asked. She edged closer to the window. Later she would pay another visit to the famed 16th century church for which the town was famous, but for now, it was enough to enjoy the sun's warmth on her face. In a couple of days, Lina would rejoin the tour group in Lviv, and she was surprised to find she was enjoying her stay with Babtsia more than she'd expected, especially since there was no television, a radio that barely worked, no washing machine or dryer and worst of all, an outhouse for a toilet.

"Linochka," Babtsia's voice rang from behind Lina's shoulder.

Lina turned to see Babtsia's puckered face looking up at her, dark, lined eyes and a toothless grin shining for the granddaughter who'd arrived from America.

Lina had been nervous about meeting her mother's mother, but Babtsia had allowed for no formalities, and before the first day of her visit was over, she'd had Lina talking about herself, drinking homemade wine, eating honey cake and laughing until the early hours of dawn. Yes, it had been a nice welcome.

Lina moved from the window to the couch where Babtsia sat waiting, a dented cardboard box clasped in her lap.

"Yes, come sit with me, Linochka," the old woman said and patted the couch next to her. "I've something to show you." There was an extra note of excitement in her grandmother's tone. "I've been waiting for the right moment," she continued. Babtsia nodded as Lina inched her body back against the red, black and white *liznyk*-covered couch that squeaked loudly. Old wire springs, which should have been taken away and put to rest long ago, sagged under the burden of extra weight.

Lina stretched her long legs out and looked over at Babtsia. "I'm ready," she announced with a smile. "Now what's so important it couldn't wait until after our walk?"

Babtsia lifted the top off the cardboard box. "Even your mother hasn't seen all of these photos," she said. "The last time she was here, the smaller cities and villages were still off-limits. I was recovering from my illness, but at least I was able to meet her in Lviv instead of having to travel all night to Kyiv."

Lina nodded, watching Babtsia's wrinkled hand sift through the stack of photos in the box, thinking of the unbearably small train compartment she'd ridden in on the way to Dobych. There'd been no ventilation, only a dirty window bolted shut inside the compartment, and Lina was reduced to sticking her head out the compartment door in order to catch a whiff of the passing breeze from a half-opened window down the corridor.

Every window inside of each compartment had also been bolted shut, Lina noted later, and only every other window out in the corridor could be opened.

"I guess they don't want anyone falling off these trains," she couldn't help muttering to herself at the time.

"Ah, Linochka," Babtsia's voice roused Lina. "There was so much I wanted to tell your mother, so much I wanted to give her. Who had time to bring all the photos?"

"But Mama only wanted to see you," Lina said, pressing a hand on Babtsia's shoulder.

Lina felt as if she ought to comfort her grandmother and soothe her the way Mama would have done if she'd been here with them. Originally, they were all supposed to come on this visit together. Even Tato, who'd had his hopes raised when Ukraine declared its sovereignty, was to come. But when Mama broke her leg three weeks before the trip, her parents decided to postpone their visit for a few months. Lina hadn't been happy about going on without them, but Babtsia had been so disappointed over the delay, barely hiding her frustration over the phone, that Lina could only reassure her grandmother that she would see her soon.

Lina ran a tentative hand down Babtsia's arm, her hand big and clumsy over the other's small frame. For some reason, she felt close to the grandmother she'd never known while growing up in America. Mama had often talked of her own mother, but her grandmother had been a part of Mama's life that Lina found hard to visualize. It was difficult to picture Babtsia walking through the streets of Ukraine, drinking tea or chatting with her neighbors while across the ocean Lina was in reality a virtual stranger to her grandmother.

It wasn't until later, after Mama had gone twice to Ukraine for a visit, that Lina began to see Babtsia as an ordinary person and not a mythic character from one of Mama's folk tales.

Lina's father didn't want Mama to go. Tato had been afraid something awful would happen to Mama, and there wouldn't be a thing he could do.

"You think the Americans will be able to intervene when the KGB picks you up," he stormed. "For God's sakes, Hania, they don't need an excuse. Your father spent 10 years in a labor camp."

He yelled so loudly that even Lina had turned pale and looked pleadingly at Mama. But Mama was determined since her baby sister Ivanka had written from Ukraine, telling her that the news wasn't good. Babtsia had been ill for months, and even the doctor wasn't sure if she'd recover.

"It's my mother," Mama's voice had been breathless but firm. "She could die, and I want to see her. I have to go. Don't you understand?" Mama had looked beseechingly at Tato.

Although Lina hadn't wanted Mama to go either, at 14, she tried to understand. "Go see your mother, but hurry home," Lina whispered as she hugged Mama at the airport.

Both times Mama returned pale and sad.

"To see what they've done to our country . . ." Mama shook her head. "Long lines stretching around the block just to buy a pressing iron or a good pair of pants. 20 years on a waiting list before you can get an apartment. And some schools don't even teach Ukrainian. It's second rate, they're told."

Lina remembered that Mama's face was tense for weeks afterward.

Babtsia moved her knees, shifting her shoulders, sweeping Lina's memory away.

Lina stilled her fingers. "It's alright now, *kohana*," Babtsia whispered, looking at her granddaughter. "You're here now. That's all that matters."

Lina nodded while Babtsia carefully lifted a stack of photos from the box and set them gently on her lap, pushing aside the dented cardboard. The sun had drifted away from the house, casting a deep shadow over the room.

Babtsia grasped the photos, picking up one after another, staring at each one for moments at a time and then setting them back on her lap, oblivious to Lina's impatient sighs at her side. At this rate, it was going to take hours to get through the photos.

"Aah, yes," Babtsia murmured, clutching a photo and turning suddenly to face her granddaughter.

"Linochka, take a look at this one," she said, her cracked lips widening, transforming her pale cheeks into small, round globes.

She is like a little girl, Lina thought and smiled as Babtsia gingerly pointed at the photo of a young woman clad in an ornate, hand-embroidered frock.

The photo was faded, musty and withered at the edges, but Lina could still see the hopeful smile in the young woman's eyes, the proud lift of her chin as she gazed forward at the camera.

"Be careful," Babtsia admonished Lina when she accidentally pressed her finger over the photo's bent surface.

"Is that you?" Lina asked, gazing from the photo to the puckered lines on her grandmother's face. Lina supposed that it had to be, yet something about the air of the young woman with the determined stare and long braids coiled around the top of her head seemed alien from the shrunken old woman seated at her side.

Lina snuck another look at her grandmother's gray head, thinning tendrils gathered tightly at the scalp and pulled back into a small bun. Her brown eyes flashed and became suddenly bright and birdlike, whereas moments before Lina had observed them to be dark and placid.

There was a snort and a shout.

"Of course it's me. Osh, child, can't you tell?" Babtsia clicked her tongue as though disappointed.

Lina fell silent, feeling she had let her grandmother down. She looked closely at the rest of the photos Babtsia pressed into her hands. It was like gazing into a time capsule, Lina thought. Everything seemed unfamiliar and foreign, like looking at snapshots from an earlier century with people standing in stilted poses, dressed in their Sunday best.

By now, Babtsia's lean figure was clearly recognizable in most of the photos, yet Lina noticed that through the years, her face reflected fewer and fewer hints of shining eyes or a confident stare. It seemed as if all the energy and laughter had been sucked out, year after year, photo after photo. Babtsia looked sad and forlorn, decided Lina, as she flipped through shot after shot and searched for any hint of joy or laughter.

There stood Babtsia with her arm around Mama's wide-eyed sister Ivanka. Babtsia with a stern-faced Dido, Mama's father who died shortly after returning from the labor camp. Babtsia with a baby in her arms, possibly Mama? Ivanka at school, standing stiffly upright, her arms hanging at her sides, face tilted downward. Even Ivanka's wedding portrait, white veil and shiny dress with not the slightest glimmer of an upturned smile.

Lina paused as she looked at shot after shot and found few signs of Mama. Before she could ask Babtsia about it, the old woman proudly pulled out a baby photo showing a girl with dark curls and a small smile. Lina recognized a slightly older Mama perched on the sloped back of a hand-carved wooden rocking horse.

There were more recent pictures of Mama after that, mostly ones sent from America, Mama smiling with Tato, and later Lina at her side. Huge smiles and bouncy cheeks with the word Kodak printed in visible letters on the back of each crisp shot.

"And what about this photo?" Babtsia grinned, motioning toward the last snapshot clutched in Lina's hand. "You recognize these people, Linochka? They look familiar, not like that stranger you saw earlier?"

"Oh, Babtsia." Lina could feel herself redden, looking down at the photo of her and her mother. It'd been taken at her high school graduation. Lina stood with her head bent close to her mother's, one arm pressed on the cap the wind flailed from side to side. It was a joyous photo even though the flying hair made it difficult for Tato to get a clear view.

Babtsia chuckled, looking down at the photo. "My little girl," she murmured softly. "All grown up and with a daughter of her own. Aah, if circumstances had been different."

"But couldn't you have escaped from the communists too?" Lina reached over and touched her grandmother's hand. "I mean, why did you let Mama go with your brother's family? Why didn't you leave too?"

Lina held her breath as Babtsia sat quietly on the couch, shoulders rigid, eyes staring forward. From the kitchen and through the ominously tense silence of the darkening room, Lina could hear the steady drip-drop of water slipping from the faucet onto the sink.

"I couldn't go," Babtsia said. Her voice rose softly over the steady sound of the water. "Ivanka was small and sickly, and your Dido refused to leave. 'What, and give up my home? Our home?' he said. 'Leave our homeland? We can outlast this war,' he said. 'And when it's finally over, we'll all be free.'"

Babtsia's bright eyes peered suddenly at Lina. "But in my heart, I wasn't convinced, Linochka," she said, gripping Lina's hand and pressing it in the moist shelter of her palms.

Lina swallowed, her eyes planted on the elderly woman's face as she continued.

"The Soviet Red Army was very close, advancing into western Ukraine. We'd just survived the Nazis, and before that we'd been under Soviet rule for two years." Babtsia paused then said, "Here in the West, our land was always being carved up by our neighbors—Austria-Hungary, Poland, Romania—we were always the second-class citizens of another country, but there were no illusions about what life under the communists would be like. Stalin's man-made famine in Eastern Ukraine was no secret to us. In any case," Babtsia said. "My brother had a house in Zakarpattia, close to the border. It was safer there, and it was only supposed to be temporary. I knew I was taking a risk but the Red Army was so close, and I wanted your Mama to be safe. She'd almost been taken away from me once already by the Nazis when they were snatching away our young and healthy ones, sending them away as forced laborers to Germany."

"Mama never told me about that," Lina said. In fact, her mother hardly ever spoke about the years during the war, and Lina wondered why she'd never pressed her mother to reveal more.

"So I sent away your Mama to Zakarpattia," Babtsia continued as if she hadn't heard. "I would have joined her, but I believed it was only temporary. The Germans were being driven out, and the Russians would be too. Everyone

aid so. Who would have thought? The Red Army came, and soon after I
eceived word from a cousin of my brother's plans. He was escaping West
vith his family and taking your mother, my Hanusia, with them. It was only
;oing to be temporary. They'd come back, my cousin reassured me. It seemed
ike the best thing to do. She was 12 then—a big girl. She deserved a chance,
ust in case. Yes, that's what I told myself."

Without warning Babtsia began rocking her body to and fro, still
:lenching Lina's hand within her own.

"But when I sent away your Mama, I didn't tell your Dido." Babtsia stilled
ler swaying and tilted her head toward Lina. "He never knew. There wasn't
ime since he'd gone away to deliver medical supplies to the partisans. But he
lever would have let her leave, not even temporarily as it was supposed to be.
Ie wouldn't have allowed it because he truly believed that we'd be living in a
'ree country after the war ended. And that evening, when his boots sounded
on the walk outside, I grew afraid because I had sent away our daughter
vithout telling him."

Babtsia released Lina's hand and pressed her palms to her face. "You'd
hink 45 years would be enough to dull the memory," she said, not looking
it Lina.

And then she went on, talking so low that Lina had to lean forward to
:atch the words.

"The door opened with a creak, and then my Vasyl's face appeared in the
ırchway, his big blue eyes darting around the room. Hanusia would always
velcome her father home with a cup of hot tea and a kiss and he'd squeeze her
n a tight embrace. But that night there was no tea, no kiss and no embrace.
Only a slight creaking as Vasyl made his way across the floor. I stood in a
:orner, holding Ivanka in my arms, and Vasyl looked questioningly at me.
First his eyes accused me silently, and then he shouted."

Lina leaned back as Babtsia raised her voice. For a second it almost
ieemed as though the older woman had forgotten her presence, but then she
vent on.

"Vasyl stomped on the floor in anger, his knees rising and falling over
ınd over. And I just watched him, silently pleading for understanding. After
ı minute he turned around and walked away. It took me a long time to realize
ıe never forgave me for it."

"What about the pictures? There's hardly any pictures of Mama," Lina

61

asked after a few minutes when she could no longer bear the silence.

"Pictures?" Babtsia laughed. "We lost most of our pictures along with everything else when the Soviets came and took away your Dido. Sometimes they'd confiscate pictures of people who fled. They were all collaborators and traitors, the communists said. But I was able to get a couple of my little Hanusia and hide them away." Babtsia's voice dropped to a whisper now. "I kept them, even after I was kicked out of our house and taken away for questioning."

Lina wondered if she should stop asking questions. Perhaps it would be better if her grandmother didn't have to recall memories that were only painful no matter which way you looked at it.

"What happened after that?" she whispered back. Lina realized she could no more stop asking Babtsia questions than her grandmother could change any of the past.

Babtsia sighed. "After the war ended, instead of getting better, it only got worse. There was no food, and almost every day someone would disappear. Later we heard that they'd been either executed or sent to the labor camps. The slam of a car door, a knock on a window and even the scrape of an unfamiliar boot against the sidewalk were enough to send you into shivers because you could never be certain they weren't coming to arrest you."

Lina wished she could say something but found that she could only stare at the way Babtsia twisted her fingers as she spoke, a gesture that Mama made every time she was upset about something. Mama never talked to Lina about the war, but Tato told her enough stories to know that few families had survived intact. At least they had survived, Tato always said. So even though Lina wasn't surprised, she was shocked by the details she discovered about Mama; details she'd never before had the slightest interest in uncovering. But her grandmother wasn't finished yet.

"Your Dido was arrested shortly after the communists took over," Babtsia said. "He was sent to Siberia for 10 years. The worst thing is, he survived the labor camp only to drop dead of a heart attack a few months after his return. They kept calling me back for questioning. Didn't I have another daughter? What happened to my brother? I told them they must have died since I'd had no news, and at the time, I actually didn't know if they'd survived or not. In the end they finally let me go but gave our house to one of their officials." Babtsia shrugged.

"The new owner didn't even wait until I got a chance to pack up all our belongings. Claimed the furniture was his now along with the house and wouldn't even let me back in to get Ivanka's favorite doll. If it wasn't for a neighbor who cleaned his house and managed to sneak out some of the family photos in some old books, I wouldn't even have these to show you today."

"Did you ever try to go back after that?" Lina asked.

Babtsia's fingers curled, and her voice sharpened. "Only once. This oaf they'd sent over stood in the doorway and told me to leave or he'd send me away like my husband. And then he laughed and said, 'I could always find a use for a woman around here if you're so attached to the place. My wife's back East, her belly swelling larger each day, so I wouldn't mind having another warm body to cuddle in the meantime. And all I remember is turning around and running as fast as I could from the house where I'd shared so many happy memories."

Lina leaned over as she stared at the darkened puffs and lines etched over her grandmother's face. She felt a bit foolish for wondering about the somber-faced photos and not recognizing her grandmother's picture in the first place. At the same time, this new-found knowledge brought her a little closer to her own mother, and she was eager to see her again. Maybe Mama still wouldn't want to talk about her past, but at least Lina could let her know she was ready to hear about it. She wasn't sure if Babtsia would really understand how much she'd given her during this visit, but on second thought, the elderly woman had a knack for surprising her.

"Forgive me," Lina whispered, planting a kiss on her grandmother's cheek.

Tricks of the Eye

On Saturday afternoons, when the noise in the upstairs flat subsides and Anna can once again hear the steady tick of the kitchen clock, she springs to her feet. Snapping her fingers, Anna goes for the broom, gripping it with the energy of a roused bulldog, banging the handle hard against the ceiling in a series of thumps.

"*Tyho*," she yells in Ukrainian. "You think a person can cook with all that racket?"

It gives her great satisfaction to shout this aloud. It hardly matters that she rarely cooks, even less that her knocks on the floor upstairs are only occasionally acknowledged. Sometimes she hears a few thumps directed back at her and then she hears muffled laughter as though the whole show was put on especially for her. In response, Anna waits for the quiet before she uses the broom.

"Let them soak up some of my noise," she mutters.

The couple upstairs is young and barely married. They've been living in Anna's house for four months now. The husband works nights at the Polish diner, and long before he's due home, Anna hears his wife pacing the floor, a frenzied click-clack from one end of the flat to another.

Anna has gone up to see her a few times, wanting to talk or better yet, be invited in for some *chai*. But after welcoming her with a big smile, Sonia always stops Anna at the door with her hand, and Anna feels her own voice falter even before she opens her mouth. Each time, she has skulked back down the stairs to her own flat.

When she'd first placed the ad for renting the flat in the church paper, she thought it'd take a long time to find another tenant she could warm to. Larysa, her former tenant, had the good grace to bring down slices of home-baked *tsvibak* every Saturday afternoon. They'd eat the pound cake together, sipping Anna's lemon tea while catching up on the gossip around the block. In the summertime, they'd move outside to the front porch, Anna craning her neck, scanning the neighborhood for any activity like a sentry at her post. They were neighbors for fifteen years. One day, Larysa brought down her usual serving of *tsvibak*, and in the same breath as her hello, announced she was moving to Cleveland to live near her sister. Never mind that Larysa hardly got along with her sister. "An old woman like me needs some change in her life," she told Anna before she left. Anna had been left to gape at an empty flat and no one to drop in on whenever she felt lonely.

Even though Anna was prepared to wait it out for the perfect tenant, she couldn't help liking the cheerful note in Sonia's voice when the phone rang a couple of weeks later.

When Sonia showed up she was alone, flustered like a child or maybe it just seemed that way to Anna. Sonia's eyes darted around, unable to settle on any one room. Suddenly worried that at the last second Sonia wouldn't take the flat after all, Anna felt compelled to pat her on the hand.

"Of course, picking the first home's a big decision," Anna said. "Just as important as planning a wedding, so you take a good look around."

Sonia rewarded her with a hearty laugh and a nod of her head. Anna then clucked over the girl as if it were her own daughter instead of a stranger come to look at the flat. She clutched Sonia's cold fingers inside her own and sped her through the rooms with an enthusiasm that'd sent a hot flush over the girl's cheeks.

* * *

Anna straightens up, puts away the broom and goes to the ornate mirror that hangs in the hall. She pats her hair, rearranging it so that the gray in her part isn't as noticeable. There's not much Anna can do about the dull color in her cheeks though; the complexion cream only makes her skin feel greasy, and besides, hers are the sort of age spots that can't be erased no matter how much powder she dabs over them. But at least her lips are still nice and full, not pinched and thin like Larysa's always were. Anna likes the way the red lipstick glides over her mouth, brightens up her face so much that sometimes she doesn't even bother with eye powder. Today though, there's a wedding at the Ukrainian church down the street, so Anna brushes bits of blue around her eyes like she did when she was young, and she and her best friend, Chrystia would go to the Saturday night *zabava* at the community dance hall. She'd been so pretty then. Even Chrystia had been jealous when Maxym Symkiw picked Anna for his dance partner.

Maxym wasn't the best dancing partner Anna ever had, but that hardly mattered in those early days when he whispered in her ear and talked about traveling to exotic places like California or Australia. Anna always dreamed of living by the ocean, ever since she was 10 years old, and her parents drove all the way from Michigan to the Jersey Shore for a weeklong vacation. She had loved the salt water and couldn't get enough of the waves, throwing herself at them as fervently as she would welcome Maxym's attentions nine years later.

She later blamed her attachment to salt water for the erosion of her common sense when it came to her marriage. Despite his protestations, she should have known Maxym had no true love of the seashore when he talked her into going to Niagara Falls for their honeymoon over Anna's preference for Cape May. Maxym's law exams were coming up shortly before the wedding, and until he had a good job, Anna agreed it made more sense to save their money. In compromise, Maxym promised her they would spend each summer vacationing on the seashore.

When they'd actually made it to the ocean, Maxym was more awkward in the water than he'd been on the dance floor. She sent him to swim lessons when they returned, which turned out to be her undoing seven months later when Maxym decided to start his life anew with one of the women in his class and moved with her to California. Anna hadn't felt the same about the seashore since.

* * *

In her neighborhood, Anna is drawn to many churches. Polish. Greek. Even Romanian. Anna's been to them all. As long as there's a wedding she can attend, that is. Over the years attending church weddings has turned into a hobby in much the same way Larysa never missed an opportunity to stop in at a funeral wake. Larysa always insisted she was only paying her respects, her high voice and uplifted eyebrows making it clear to Anna that weddings were an entirely separate matter.

"People are invited to weddings, Anna," she'd say. "But no one objects when you're there to share in their grief."

"Especially when you barely know the family," Anna flung back, but then she'd let the matter drop before Larysa started in on the dough birds Anna baked for these occasions.

St. Olha's, the Ukrainian church with an immense gold dome towering over the rest of the block, is where Anna worships. Inside, colorful painted icons dance across the ceilings and sides of the church, and Anna usually slips into one of the back pews and sits there, twisting her fingers. She loves the smell of incense, overpowering as it is, loves to watch all the colors on the paintings sparkle like a kaleidoscope when the sun streams through the high windows on Sunday mornings. Although for a long time after Maxym left her, Anna didn't feel as if she belonged anywhere, even here with the Virgin Mary gazing down at her from the inside of the dome, arms outstretched like she was about to fold Anna in a tight embrace. But even then Anna couldn't help being awed by that peaceful gaze and those curved lips, those eyes, smiling almost, that stared at her from above.

Back when she and Maxym were married, she knew everyone who attended Sunday Mass, some making the drive into the city from 20 miles away. These days, it's mostly new immigrants who fill up the pews. When she sits in on weddings, nobody says anything to her, not in the church while she's standing with her head up, straight and staring ahead, so rapt that everyone thinks she's a close friend. Sometimes she will get a couple of glances, if it's a small wedding especially, but Anna doesn't mind the stares. She's here to look at the bride, from the second she first walks down the carpeted aisle and sweeps past Anna in a blur of white chiffon, casting off a sweet-smelling scent like one of those perfume samples Anna sometimes gets at the department store cosmetics counter.

It's important to look at the bride's face just before she goes down the aisle, and that's why Anna sits at the end of the pew, studies her expression and the way she stands, hands clenched around a bouquet, and especially her eyes as she glides past. The eyes are what Anna likes to look at the most. When they're shiny and glittery, Anna lets a small sigh escape. But the skittish ones that bounce from side to side, taking in everything around them like a ping pong ball, those girls, with looks of stifled apprehension, remind Anna of her own misgivings on her wedding day.

* * *

With her hair securely clipped in place, the upswept *fryzura*, as Larysa always called it, and a shiny white handbag clamped over her shoulder, Anna is ready to attend today's wedding at St. Olha's. The dough birds she's baked for the bride and groom are already tucked away in a white handkerchief right next to the five dollars Anna will spend on lottery tickets after the ceremony is over. The birds represent the bride and groom and are supposed to bring good luck. At Ukrainian weddings, they're placed on the traditional wedding bread called the *korovai* along with a tree of life and other dough ornaments. Anna bakes birds for all the wedding ceremonies she attends, regardless of the couple's background. The way she sees it, a little extra good luck won't hurt anyone, and besides, maybe if they'd had dough birds on her wedding *korovai*, she and Maxym might still be together.

Anna grabs her keys, but then stops, tapping her foot as loud music pulsates from her tenants' flat above. Ordinarily she would stick around, pacing her kitchen floor, then sit impatiently by the clock until there'd be a lull in the noise, prodding her into action. It's not so much that Anna minds the music, although she'd prefer Vivaldi over the sound of drums and screams. It's just that Anna would enjoy hearing how these two met in the first place. She wants to look around their apartment, study the photos they've propped up on the dresser, but every month Sonia slips the rent check under her door before Anna has a chance to ask her in.

Sometimes the aroma of fresh baked cookies fills the hall, and Anna will open her door, mouth watering, but Sonia hasn't brought down a plate since the one time Anna had invited her in and then spent a full two hours showing Sonia her old photographs. She'd always assumed Sonia baked the cookies until the day Sonia had walked in through the front door, gone up the stairs, and Anna heard her chuckle as she caught the whiff of *medivnychky*. So he was the one baking for her, Roman or Rostyk, she never remembered which. Anna couldn't remember Maxym ever baking for her. Even when she'd been sick, Maxym had been more helpless than helpful, scorching the *rosyl* her mother cooked for her.

* * *

It's a cool day for a late May wedding but Anna takes her time walking down the street past all her neighbors' homes. There aren't many old-timers left in the neighborhood. Those who haven't died moved to the suburbs, and the newcomers seem to have more friends drop by than they know what to do with. It was the same for her when she and Maxym were first married, and even later when Anna got back on her feet after the divorce. She'd had a few suitors over time, but by then was used to being on her own. But now with the young couple living upstairs, Anna finds herself rethinking her married days. When Larysa was around, there'd been no time to think much about her past, although Larysa often scolded her about making dough birds for strangers.

"This obsession with weddings is bad enough," Larysa would say. "But to pass out birds like confetti... You know they call you the bird lady."

Anna laughed it off, but secretly she'd been flattered by the label. Better to be remembered for something than to be overlooked like a drab frock. And Anna liked to bake the birds, likening it to a part-time profession.

In her case, the dough birds had been left off her *korovai* inadvertently, but it was hardly surprising, considering she'd almost called off her own wedding at the last minute.

She'd met Maxym the summer she turned 20 and had just cut her hair. She and her friend Chrystia were nearly inseparable until the Saturday night Maxym gripped Anna's hands, led her onto the dance floor and they'd twirled around the room, lagging behind the other couples. Even now Anna still remembers the feel of Maxym's hand tight against her back.

When he proposed, her father thought she was too young, but her mother had shushed him saying, "He's a good boy. Studying to be a lawyer." And her father had turned away, shrugging his shoulders.

A few weeks before the wedding, Anna found out that Maxym cheated on some tests to get into law school. That's when she'd thought about calling it all off, but Maxym pleaded until Anna couldn't think straight anymore. Then he said he'd retake the tests and her mother called her in for a dress fitting, and Anna allowed herself to think it'd be all right in the end.

Before this incident, she'd never obsessed about little details when it came to Maxym, but now Anna found herself analyzing their conversations for hidden messages, scrutinizing his friends' faces and words to see if other, even more unscrupulous secrets would be revealed. Ultimately, Anna allowed herself to be convinced, and so she listened to Maxym talk about their future, his eyes glinting in the way she remembered from the start of their courtship.

Afterward, it was hard to precisely recall what Maxym said to her, but when Anna stepped through the archway of St. Olha's on her wedding day, she knew her passion for Maxym would never be as strong as at that moment when all the guests stared at her with broad smiles. Armed with this knowledge, Anna walked down the aisle with Maxym at her side, per Ukrainian tradition. She did not pause even as she passed her parents in the ront pew although she noted tears on one face and smiles on the other.

* * *

Inside St. Olha's church, there's the usual air of expectation right before he ceremony begins. The pews are especially packed today, and Anna can lear the choir shuffling around and whispering in the balcony. *They're like* *:hildren, really*, Anna thinks, pursing her lips when she hears the conductor ;ive them instructions for the opening song. The women are bad enough alking and tittering all through his directive, but it's the shuffling of papers ınd feet that are especially loud and echo down to the pews. Why, if it was ıer up there, she'd have the choir under control in no time. And then Anna ·emembers that there's a new conductor on the premises, a young man with a ·ong mustache who talks about bringing a modern touch to the music. Anna ,vas quite happy with the old conductor, who recently retired, and wonders f she'll have to complain to the priest if the singing gets too out of hand. Maxym always told her she was a good, strong-minded girl with her own ;pecific sense of taste, but it took a long time for her to figure out it wasn't ıecessarily a positive thing in his eyes.

He was like that though—always thinking one thing and saying another. By the time Anna caught on to it, it didn't matter all that much. All the crying ;he'd done in the first year of the marriage dissipated overnight as though a .imit was reached and she was suddenly bound to new rules of play.

"Are these seats taken?" A woman with a large white hat and two children ıt her side startles Anna with a touch on the shoulder. Anna shudders, not so much from the intrusion but because she realizes that the white handkerchief with the dough birds is still inside her purse instead of being safely tucked ınto the best man's pocket or the flower girl's basket. Anna makes it a habit to present her little offering before the ceremony begins, but today she'd arrived :arlier than usual and didn't keep close tabs on the wedding party.

Anna turns toward the back but it's too late. Even the choir's gone quiet. There's such a hush that it's hard to believe anyone's even up there. Then the palatial-looking gold doors at the front of the church open and a priest :merges with a cross in one hand. He strides down the aisle toward the back of the church. Anna is so distracted by the thought of the dough birds that she pulls out the handkerchief from her purse and clutches it in her hand. She :an hardly keep still after that, but she turns toward the entrance along with :veryone else.

The groom, round-faced and sweaty, stands beside the bride, shifting his shoulders. At first, Anna only gives him a cursory glance, doesn't see that he's holding his breath and his cheeks are red, even more red than the rouge the bride has brushed over her own face. Instead Anna looks at the dark-haired bride, whose face is solemn, her gaze set on the priest who's arrived to bless them and lead them up to the altar.

The priest is standing there so close to the bride that Anna has to practically lean out into the aisle so she can look into her eyes. She can't even get a clear view because of the veil and string of pearls hanging low over her forehead. That's when Anna looks back at the groom and she can see Maxym mirrored there so clearly, it's a wonder she missed it at first glance. Hadn't he also fidgeted like a restless boy who longed to be outside and wanted to just fly, fly through the fields to the makeshift fort in the woods? In the wedding pictures, his smile always seemed a bit too wide, the pose a degree too stiff. Maybe he'd wanted to duck out the door on their wedding day and start out fresh with someone more forgiving about the little things, if not the big ones. He hadn't, though. He'd cracked small jokes as they went up the aisle and steadied her hand when it shook as she slipped the wedding band onto his finger. He'd kissed her so long and hard when the ceremony was over that even the priest had burst out laughing.

For all his stiffness on the dance floor and his stiffness in the water, it was Anna who was too unwilling to bend in the marriage. Maybe if they were able to have that baby they wanted so much, it would have all turned out differently in the end. Maybe then she could have forgiven the tests Maxym never got around to retaking. It was hard to say how any of it could have been better, or perhaps even worse, but Anna is saved from further speculation when the woman in the white hat standing next to her unexpectedly takes Anna's hand in hers.

"It is beautiful, isn't it? The most beautiful thing in the world," the woman says.

Anna licks her dry lips, unwittingly crushing the dough birds with her fingers, her eyes as moist as her own father's had been on her wedding day. Maybe she's been wrong about the dough birds all along. Hadn't her mother squeezed two birds into her hands at the wedding reception right before their first toast? The insistent grip of the woman standing next to her brings back the recollection Anna was so willing to forget. Or has she simply conjured up an imaginary memory? Anna tries to say something but finds that she can only clear her throat in response, and so she returns the firm pressure of the woman's grip, squeezes her hand even tighter, holding on like it's her life on the line before she'll allow her fingers to loosen, her hand to slide away slowly, before, finally, Anna allows herself to let go.

The Bell Tower

Darkness came quickly to Roznitiv. This was particularly true in winter, when after five o'clock even the dogs crept stoically back to their yards and settled themselves by the lights that glowed like beacons from inside each house. The silhouette of the nearby Carpathian mountains encircled the town, making the night seem foreboding to the occasional visitor, but to Petro Krawchuk, who had often trudged through the woods into the mountains, the winter darkness proved more welcome than a summer's warmth.

It was easier to mask one's actions when those with curious eyes were more concerned with staying warm inside their houses. *And yet*, Petro thought with a grimace, his breath shallow and quick, *curious eyes flourished in all seasons, hot and cold.*

Tonight, though, was especially chilly, and Petro pulled the collar up around the nape of his neck, the wind hitting his face like a lash, his fingers tingling inside the worn cloth of his gloves. He didn't have far to go now. The priest's house was on the outskirts, and Petro left the town lights behind, his stride long and forceful on the snow-covered ground.

The house, rundown now, with paint chipping off the sides and cracks on the stairs, was built long before Petro was born. As a child, Petro played with the children who lived there. He even sat behind the long oak table in the dining room, eating apple dumplings and drinking *kvas*. But that was in the years before the war. The family, long gone now, left everything behind and fled West, weeks before the Soviet Red Army occupied the town. He'd later heard that they'd made it to Canada, although it was something that was spoken of quietly in whispers that snaked through the town.

Petro reached the house and looked around, noting the empty roadway, the moon half hidden by clouds, before knocking softly on the door. There

79

was movement inside, and then Father Markian's round whiskered face peered out through a window. Almost instantly the door swung open, and with a wave of his brown-spotted hand, the priest beckoned Petro inside.

"You're out late tonight," Father Markian nodded, his gray eyebrows lifting, eyes scanning Petro's face.

"Needed some fresh air, Father," Petro replied, rubbing his palms together. He then followed the priest into the small kitchen.

Petro stood in the archway. His eyes darted over the two pots on the stove, the wooden bowl on the counter, the flowerpot on the sill in an opposite corner, and the loaf of bread already drying at the edges placed on a plate in the center of the table. Old Murka was curled up on the floor underneath the table not even flickering an eye at Petro's arrival. She'd usually come sauntering out with her head high then prance on the cupboard ledge before finally jumping and settling comfortably into Petro's lap.

"Marta will be by tomorrow with some *makivnyk*," Petro smiled at the priest. "She knows how much you like it."

"She's a good woman, that Marta." Father Markian's eyes brightened, adding softness to the grizzled face. "Well, sit down, Petro," he said as he waved a hand at a chair. "You didn't come over here to stand in the doorway."

Petro sat down. He wondered how quickly he'd be able to leave and how fast he could get what he came for.

As it turned out, he didn't have to wait long. Father Markian, busy at the stove with his back turned, was mechanically stirring the *borsch* simmering in the pot.

Petro stood up, surprised to find that his hands trembled while he made his way to the window, feigning an interest in the night. Just like he remembered, the key was hidden in the flower pot, resting in the dirt not far from the top. The priest once showed him the hiding place and Petro wondered how many others had been let in on the secret. In any case, hiding the key didn't seem important since the church was shut down years ago, but Petro knew that the priest kept the key around, just in case.

"It's been so long," Father Markian's voice startled Petro, and he stepped away from the window, the soiled key clamped in his palm. "Seems a lifetime ago," the priest said, his gnarled fingers grasping the edge of the wooden spoon and moving it in circular motions through the stewing chunks of beets.

"So long since what, Father?" asked Petro, brushing the dirt from the key onto his pants, then slipping it into the pocket of his dark brown coat. "Since we all gathered openly, you mean? And yet if it wasn't for your courage, your example, where would we be? Father, you…"

"Stop that." The rebuke came sharply. "I've done no more than the others. I should have been there last month in the forest near Heryn. Not Father Taras. I know the woods better than he does. He's still young, impatient for change. Perhaps too impatient. Too trusting. But I thought I was being watched and let him go alone."

"Any word?" Petro asked softly.

"Still under arrest along with 20 others. And who knows how they found out this time." The priest's shoulders sagged, cheeks crumpling into folds.

Petro moved quietly around. His hand touched the priest's shoulder. They'd been friends for a long time now. Petro was one of the few who wrote letters to him when Father Markian was taken away and imprisoned. The official charge had been spreading anti-Soviet propaganda, a label Petro knew had been conveniently used to arrest hundreds, if not thousands.

"However slowly, times are changing now, Markian. You must believe that," Petro said, tightening his grip on the priest's shoulder.

Father Markian sighed as he lifted the spoon to his lips and tasted, swirling the soup slightly around in his mouth.

"I suppose you're right," he finally acknowledged. "Of all people, I mustn't lose hope. It's just that lately I've been feeling old, Petro, very old."

Petro smiled at the rueful look in the priest's eyes and chuckled. "Don't we all, Father?"

The two men looked at each other and laughed, Petro's face creased and ruddy from the cold outside, Father Markian's pale and lined, yet their voices fused into a chortle, startling the sleeping Murka as the cat let out a resounding meow.

* * *

Petro left the priest's house and quickly walked along the dark road, fingering the key in his pocket and darting a glance over his shoulder. Fortunately, Father Markian was too worried about the recent arrests to pay close attention to Petro. Otherwise, Petro knew it wouldn't have been so easy to leave, since normally the old priest would insist on accompanying him.

The church was located about a half a mile down the road, just past the bend, and Petro wanted to get there before Marta noticed he was missing.

She would still be at the neighbor's, he thought, making *torte* and laughing with Roma over the kitchen table, two plump faces huddled together like schoolgirls, and every once in a while a wild cackle would emerge, and they would grin at each other as though they'd just been let in on some well-kept secret.

But Marta didn't laugh yesterday. When he'd mentioned getting hold of the key to open up the church, she set in on him like a snapping dog, slamming the plate of potato pancakes down in front of him with a bang, her bushy eyebrows lifting and her wide mouth crinkling in disapproval when she noted Petro's set countenance.

"It's no good," she said as she sat down on the other end of the oak table and glared across at her husband.

"There's no point in stirring up trouble, Petro," she repeated. "Leave things alone."

"Things have been left alone for too long. And now they want to tear down the church altogether. Is that what you want, Marta?" Petro asked as he leaned across the table. His gray locks fell over his forehead and his fists gripped the edge of the white tablecloth.

He looked intently at Marta. Her eyes fell as she twisted a napkin between her right forefinger and thumb.

"We've left things alone for too long. Maybe if we had acted sooner, our own son wouldn't have turned against us."

"Enough Petro," Marta hissed, raising her eyes in anger.

But Petro only shook his head, lifting his fork to his lips.

* * *

The church was set back from the unpaved roadway, and Petro stepped carefully through the mounds of snow that enclosed the building from all sides. It'd been years since Petro even set foot inside the little church, but after some trouble with the key, he pushed open the door with the ease of a man who hadn't been away for a single day. Surefooted and quick, he locked the door from the inside, letting his eyes adjust to the darkness for several seconds before pulling out a candle and matches, dropping the key into his pocket. Petro's fingers, unexpectedly stiff and awkward, fumbled, nearly dropping the matches onto the floor before finally lighting one on the fifth try. To the left of him, the candlelight revealed planks which had been nailed over a window, the wood now splintered, creating a jagged gap, admitting cold from the air outside.

The stairs were at the other side of the church and Petro moved slowly through the center aisle, clenching the candle tightly in his numb fingers while thrusting his feet forward. His worn brown boots crunched on the mishmash of pebbles and shards of glass scattered across the floor, and Petro wheezed, dust engulfing his face.

The staircase was steep and narrow, and gripping the wooden beam that served as a banister, Petro eased his way up. The planks creaked heavily under his weight while Petro shifted his bulky frame from one step to the next.

"Ready to fall apart and still they're afraid. Even to let us inside," he muttered under his breath, dirt and grime from the banister settling onto his hand and sleeve, staining the coat Marta had so carefully cleaned for him earlier that day.

Marta would probably be home soon, Petro thought, her light step echoing up the walk, her keys jiggling as she swung them around in her hand. There was nothing simple about Marta's walk. Precise maybe but never simple. Her feet always moved in little half-steps and Petro used to tease her about going off in her own little dance while the rest of the world walked by in ordinary strides. But she would only toss back her head, lower her chin and swagger around. She said it was an imitation of Petro's walk, and even he would have to laugh at her agile steps.

Marta had been dancing since she was four, and it didn't stop even after Stefan was born. Many times in those early years, Petro would come in on the two of them, and Marta would have the baby pressed against her breast, whirling around the room in little circles while Stefan laughed and screamed for more.

Maybe we should have had more children, Petro thought. It might have helped, especially lately, if they had something else to look at across the table other than each other's forlorn faces. But then after what happened with Stefan, Petro was almost glad that they didn't have more children who could come and look them straight in the eye and calmly tell them that everything they believed in was nothing more than a big hoax. It was enough to make a man put a bottle to his lips and never want to put it down. But after a while Petro did, and then he just tried to pretend that it had been only him and Marta from the start.

Petro sighed, breathing heavily when he reached the top of the stairs, his body freezing as the silence in the church was cut short by shouts outside. It was probably Marta, Petro thought, and he held his breath to listen for the sound of pounding on the door downstairs. He imagined her telling him to stop being a fool, to come back down the stairs, open the church door and take her home. *Go home, Marta*, Petro silently pleaded. *Tonight one fool's more than enough.*

The shouting grew louder, and now Petro could make out several voices and then a burst of singing. Petro chuckled, relieved. It wasn't Marta after all. Just some locals having a little fun on their way home. After a few minutes the voices faded and Petro moved away from the stairs and into the room.

Large, taped-up cartons were scattered throughout, and Petro moved around them, lowering his head to avoid the low-ceilinged beams and heading straight for the bell tower. Petro blew out the candle when he reached the bell. Then he grasped one end of a rotting wooden plank in his hand, and with the other, unraveled the long rope hooked around it. The rope was tightly wound and looked like it hadn't been untwined in years, so Petro took his time lightly brushing his quivering fingers over the strand before letting it slide to the ground. He kept his eyes trained on the bell, which was perched solidly on the belfry, and although the moon illuminated his surroundings, Petro wished he had brought along a lantern. Looking down, he noticed a stack of children's books lying on the floor.

If he didn't know better, he would have sworn that those were Stefan's old books left behind from the days when Stefan played in the bell tower while Petro and Marta swept up the floor or tended to the flower garden outside. But like Stefan himself, those old books were long gone, and now Petro could only scan the darkness, wondering who had gotten in without the key after all his trouble earlier tonight. *Despite the cold weather, there seems to be an abundance of activity tonight*, Petro thought, more irritated than apprehensive. He looked around and grew more annoyed by the second. Just when he thought no one was there after all, Petro spotted a young girl crouched behind one of the cartons on the other side of the room.

"Don't you know that hiding up here is dangerous? If those planks give way no one would even know to help you," Petro said.

"What are you doing here if it's so dangerous?" she replied.

Petro peered through the darkness trying to get a better look at the girl. At one time he used to know all the children in the neighborhood. At one time

84

heir house had been the destination of choice—if it wasn't Stefan's friends, it
vas Marta's *tistochky*, which she baked every morning and then invited the
hildren to stop by and eat each afternoon.

"Come over here where I can take a look at you," commanded Petro,
traightening his shoulders, his tone intentionally gruff.

The girl made no response, and Petro turned back to the rope. It was late.
He didn't have any time to waste. "Suit yourself," he said. "I'll just get on with
my work then."

"You're not with the *militsia*, are you?" she asked minutes later as if
hey were engaged in casual conversation all along and the thought had just
occurred to her.

"No. I'm just an old man," Petro said. "You can come out now. You don't
have to hide from me."

Tiny black boots encased on thin, elf-like feet emerged hesitantly from
behind the carton, and Petro had to stifle a grin at the almost comical figure
hat stood before him.

"Well, what are you laughing at?" muttered the girl, who couldn't be more
han 13 years old.

Petro's eyes moved from the pointed buckled boots to the red, dirt-
smudged trousers, up to the ruffly blouse covered with a plaid scarf. Finally
his gaze settled on the pale face that was masked by curls of blonde hair before
shaking his head slowly.

"Listen *dytynko*, shouldn't you be at home?" he asked. "Your mother and
father must be wondering what's keeping you."

The girl's eyes darted across the room before resting on the rope that
Petro still clutched in his hand.

"But they mustn't know," she said. Just for a second, her voice reminded
Petro of Marta as she'd restrained his hand forcefully, and brought it down to
his side before he could hit Stefan flat across the face when he came home a few
weeks earlier. It was only for her sake that he submitted as Stefan stood there
white-faced and pursing his lips. He walked in when Petro and Marta were
eating dinner, a strange grin on his face as he played with the house key in his
hand. It had been months since Stefan had come home from the university,
and Marta jumped and ran toward her son while he stood stiffly in her grasp.

"What's wrong, Stefan?" she asked when he made no effort to return her
embrace.

85

"I'm leaving for Moscow. They've accepted my credentials. I'll be starting at the bottom, of course," he said and then paused as Marta's arms dropped and Petro's glass fell to the floor, shattering in fragments near his feet.

In the silence that followed, Petro could only see the little boy with light curly hair sitting quietly by his side as he recounted stories from Ukrainian history, while nearby, Marta stood and twisted her hands nervously. "Careful Petro," she would warn. "Even the walls in this country have ears." As if it even mattered in the long run.

"You can't be serious. Working for the KGB." Petro rose to his feet, hands ground into fists. "We didn't spend all those years raising you so that you could come and spit in our faces."

Stefan blanched, biting his lip, yet stood his ground, arms glued to his sides even as Petro moved toward him.

"What are you thinking, Stefan? Are you going to arrest your own neighbors for attending religious services or speaking their minds?"

"They'll be tearing them down soon. The local churches. Even the one here," Stefan said, ignoring the question. "The talk is they'll be doing it after the New Year. It's been abandoned for years anyway," Stefan went on, as Marta grabbed the edge of the couch to steady herself. "Mama, be sensible," he turned to her. "Can't you see this is the only way for me to have a good future?"

Stefan moved toward his mother then, but Petro got there first, and if Marta hadn't straightened up and held his hand back, he would have struck his own son. He would have hit him with a strength he didn't even know he had. He would have hit the son he'd never had to raise a hand to in 21 years.

"Leave now. We can talk when you've come to your senses," Marta said, the edge in her voice brooking no refusal, and it was only after Stefan slammed the door shut that Petro and Marta fell into each other's arms. They held each other as though they were about to be separated, as if they didn't know if they'd ever see one another again.

"Are you listening to me?" The girl's voice jolted Petro to the present. "I've been coming here for months."

"You've been getting in through that window, haven't you?"

The girl nodded. "This is where I can get away from all their fighting. I get along better with Mama. At least she doesn't yell as much as Tato."

Petro looked at her and wished he could give her something. Something she'd never forget no matter how many years went by. Something he never was able to pass on to his son. But it was an impossible task and Petro knew it. "It's important for people to hear the bell ringing from this church tonight," he said. He hoped she would understand it someday, if not now. "Tomorrow will be Christmas Eve."

"But this church has been shut down for years now."

"That's right," Petro said. "This bell has been silenced for way too long. You've never heard it ringing, have you?"

"No, Tato yells at Mama if she even brings up the old traditions. So now she doesn't say a word about them. But he still shouts at her anyway."

Petro lifted his hand, almost as if to cross over and hug her, but he restrained the impulse, turning his attention back to the bell. By now, Marta would have returned home and might this very moment be heading for the church. Or she could be at home staring at Stefan's photograph, the way she stared at it every night, pulling it out from inside the dresser when she thought Petro was asleep. Petro knew from other relatives that Stefan was still in the area, and he wondered what his son would do when he heard the ringing, or if he'd even guess it was his father up here.

"You're going ahead, aren't you?" the girl asked when Petro finished unraveling the rope.

"I have to," Petro replied, glancing at her.

"You really think it'll make any difference?"

Petro smiled. "You know my wife and I were married here. It was a late summer day. Not too hot, not too cold. We weren't sure what to expect since that time of year is so unpredictable. Marta had on a beautiful dress that day, but all I remember is how her eyes kept looking at me. She wasn't nervous at all, not about the ceremony or our future either, even though her father wasn't too enthusiastic about me. 'Just listen to your heart. That's all you can do,' she told me."

Petro pulled the rope, muscles straining. It was harder than he remembered, working the rope up and down, back and forth, trying to find the precise rhythm, his hands feeble, then stronger, the rope slippery, then coarse. He forgot all about the girl until she moved next to him.

"There's still time." Petro bobbed his head. "Go on, get out of here."

But the girl didn't move. "What will happen to you?" she asked.

For a moment Petro let his fingers slip from the rope as he grasped the young girl's hand in his.

"My name's Lada Danchyk," she said, squeezing his hand in response before turning away toward the door.

The bell was chiming for at least ten minutes before the first sounds of *militsia* cars were heard through the darkness. By that time, loud, resonant tolls had swept from house to house, echoing into the surrounding woods and beyond.

Crossroads

Lesia eyes the unopened letter resting on the kitchen table and thinks about her husband Ostap back home in Vorivka, which is an ocean and more miles away than she can fathom, even when she puts her finger on a map and traces the long route she traveled to get from Western Ukraine to Michigan. Ostap's handwriting is big and loops in all directions, curls across the entire width of the envelope. If she didn't know better, she'd think the handwriting belonged to a schoolboy instead of a reserved 42-year-old dentist.

She's had his letter for a week now, and even though she can imagine him at his desk, barefooted and bare-chested, writing to her in the middle of the night, Lesia isn't ready to read the words. Although the topic of divorce didn't actually surface during their last telephone conversation when Lesia told Ostap she wasn't sure when she'd be coming home, the silence over the line was more striking than if they'd actually spoken the word aloud.

Lesia's not sure what she wants, although she's pretty certain Ostap wants to make a clean break and start his life all over again. Wasn't that why he'd had an affair in the first place? Sure, he took her in his arms and talked about moving past it until Lesia had told him to stop. She felt like she was standing in the middle of the rushing *Prut* River, and no matter which way she'd turn, the slippery rocks sent her tumbling to her knees. All Lesia wanted to do was maintain her balance in the situation and try to forget that her husband had cheated on her with one of his old girlfriends; his former fiancée, no less. Ostap might have thought Lesia could forgive him as quickly as the tryst ended, but all Lesia could wonder about was when Ostap would be tempted to betray her again.

Maybe it was a blessing she'd been so busy packing and making arrangements for her trip so that when she found out about the affair, she

91

hadn't had much time to think about making any long-term decisions. Money was scarce in Vorivka. Opportunities were even scarcer, and months earlier, when an old friend of her aunt's offered to employ her as a nanny and housekeeper, Lesia and Ostap knew they were luckier than most of their neighbors and accepted the offer.

During her 10 months living in America, Lesia learned how to drive a car, how to smile at the cashiers and blurt out a few short sentences in English when she's told to have a nice day, how to say she's doing fine when she's spent half the night worrying about her teenage sons in Ukraine and the other half wondering if her husband Ostap ever loved her in the first place. Lesia has also learned that in her marriage, planned or unplanned, right or wrong, infidelity is no longer an exclusive matter.

Just then, the phone rings, and when Lesia answers, Mykola, the other man in her life, tells her he's won $1,000 on a lottery ticket. His voice is loud and happy, like a child who's been told he can pick out any toy in the store, and soon Lesia is laughing too, laughing so hard at Mykola's luck that she's gasping for breath until Mykola spoils it all by asking her about Ostap's letter.

"What are you waiting for?" Mykola asks. "It's not like his letter's going to change anything, is it?"

"I can't talk right now, not over the phone like this," Lesia says, and her voice, normally soft and even, crackles like a light bulb that's about to dim.

Mykola lets out a groan. "Forget I said anything," he finally says. "I just wanted to tell you about the lottery ticket."

* * *

That night, Lesia picks up the telephone and dials the 15-digit code to Ukraine. It's seven hours ahead in Vorivka, just on the brink of dawn, but Ostap is an early riser and is probably at this moment stretching his legs out on the bed, already thinking about his morning coffee. She suddenly realizes that it's the boys' voices she wants to hear, the twins she wants to hold in her arms, even though they're almost 15 and adept at telling her they're much too old for a mother's hugs. She always wanted to have a third child, a girl she could take to the ballet and dress up in *kokardy*, but Ostap laughed and told her the twins were more than enough to handle. When Lesia insisted, he didn't protest, but after a couple of years went by without any luck, Lesia had simply let the matter drop.

"Allo."

Ostap answers the phone just like Lesia knew he would, and she lets him figure out that it's her on the other end.

"Did you get my letter?" He doesn't even bother with any of the preliminaries.

"How are the boys?" she asks.

Ostap sighs. "They think you're coming home in the summer when the visa expires."

"You know we need the money."

"I know we do." Ostap pauses. "That's not it, though, is it?"

Lesia taps her fingers against the phone, not wanting to give him an answer. She can't keep silent for long though.

"You're going to have to stop thinking about the past sometime," Ostap says. "It's only going to eat at you."

"Stop giving me advice," she snaps. "When I want your opinion, I'll ask for it."

"Don't be mad. I'll get the boys." Ostap softens. "They miss you. They're planning to paint the entire house for your return."

Lesia longs for him to say more; to tell her how a husband needs a wife by his side; to tell her she's being foolish to consider staying in a country where she has no legal rights; to tell her that he's the biggest fool in the world for letting her go in the first place. But Ostap doesn't say another word, and then Lesia can hear Yura and Taras laughing together on the other end, each one grabbing the receiver from the other's hands.

"Mama, Taras is in a band now," Yura says. "You remember how he used to scare all the girls away when he'd start singing at school? Well, now you can hear them shriek in horror even before he opens his mouth."

"He's just jealous as always," Taras says, grabbing the receiver. "He wants to be in the band so bad, he's learning to play guitar."

It's their antics and loud laughter that make Lesia chuckle, and for a second she's right there next to them, all those unfathomable miles dissipated in one breath. When they ask about her return to Ukraine, Lesia follows Ostap's lead and doesn't tell them she's reconsidering her plans. There's no point in upsetting them until she decides for certain. Lesia talks to the boys for a long time and when Ostap finally comes back on the line, Lesia is so happy that she jokes with her husband as though they've only been separated for a couple of days. Even Ostap seems caught up in the moment and doesn't mention the letter again until the end of their conversation.

"You can't put things off forever," he says. "Decisions need to be made. Life here is chaotic enough as it is."

"Stop right there," Lesia says. "Can't we just have a normal phone conversation? Is that too much to ask?"

She puts the phone down as soon as she can after that, barely giving Ostap the chance to say good-bye.

* * *

When the twins were small, Lesia would chase them around the house, then gather them to her side before allowing them to escape her embraces and run outside.

"You're spoiling them," Ostap always told her when he'd come home at night and they'd still be running around the neighborhood, dinner cold on the table and the boys nowhere to be found.

"Let them be," she'd say, drumming her fingers on the counter, although many times she wouldn't say anything at all, content to just ladle the soup into his bowl and move around the kitchen like a firefly, hands and feet quickening with each motion until the boys would burst through the door and they'd all sit down at the table.

She met Ostap at her cousin's wedding when she was barely 17 years old. He was shy around her although he was six years older and had already been engaged until his fiancée broke their engagement and married another man. Olya Marchuk had been Ostap's first love, and everyone who knew them expected them to get married. It probably started around the time they were both 10 years old and were dance partners in the *Maky* children's folk troupe. Or it could have been from the time Ostap fell from a tree in *Pan* Burda's orchard and Olya had run two miles in record time to get the doctor. In any case, their parents made wedding plans by the time Ostap was getting ready for his two-year mandatory service in the Soviet Army. They planned to be married when he returned, but by then Olya was expecting a child with her new husband.

Lesia found out about it all later, after Ostap kissed her in the backyard of her parents' house. He pressed her tight against his chest and rubbed his fingers against her neck in circles until Lesia pulled his fingers to her mouth, kissing each one in turn.

Ostap wasn't the first boy she'd kissed, but he was the only one who left her ightheaded, her fingers clutching his back as if they had a mind of their own. t didn't take her long to fall in love, and when he'd asked her to marry him iix months later, Lesia hesitated only a moment, for the first time bringing ip his previous engagement. Ostap told Lesia he loved her now and the past)elonged in the past. Having no reason to doubt him, she whispered yes into iis ear.

These days, when Lesia allows herself to think about Ostap's affair, she :an't help but remember what he told her that night in the dark—how the)ast belonged in the past. It's probably what she resents the most, how Ostap)icked up the old threads in his life and interweaved them with the present like i mismatched *vyshyvka*. Even though they had some rough patches before, ⸀esia isn't sure they can mend things this time around. Ostap talks so much ibout practicalities, he forgot Lesia loves to get hometown newspapers in the nail from him or hear about how much he misses her walnut *torte*. Nearly wo decades of marriage, and he still doesn't understand that she needs to ʾocus on the little things before she can move on to the big ones.

* * *

Sunday is her day off, and Lesia pulls on her boots and dons her sheepskin ⸀ozyh before heading out the door. For some reason Lesia feels completely :omfortable here, although at first glance, this neighborhood doesn't resemble ier village in the least. There are cars parked in front of every house for itarters, while in Vorivka, you'd be pressed to find more than a handful at any ʒiven time. She misses the neighborhood dogs that roam freely back home. Here they're all chained up or let loose on a patch of grass—backyards, they're :alled, but in reality there's not enough room for a good game of hide-and-ieek, even for the little ones. The neighbors are friendly though and smile ind wave as she walks past, and maybe that's why there's more of that village itmosphere than she'd expected.

The Ukrainian church is only a couple of blocks away, and Lesia walks hrough the snow-covered streets at a brisk pace, past the two-story houses vith cracked steps that belong to immigrants who ended up in this city which ias seen better days. Of course that's what she's been told by the people who ived here for decades, like *Pani* Slava, whose house Lesia cleans when she's iot taking care of her landlady's two-year-old twin granddaughters. She nvited Lesia into her home and gave her a job all because she and Lesia's aunt vere like sisters in the days before the war. Her landlady lives downstairs, and

Lesia has the whole upstairs apartment to herself. When *Pani* Slava pries into Lesia's personal life, she does it with a smile, inviting Lesia's confidences with a touch of her hand.

"*Moya doroha*," *Pani* Slava says, fixing Lesia with a look as though she's known her since the day she was born. "Tell me how you met Ostap."

Lesia finds it surprisingly easy to talk to her landlady. Maybe it's the way *Pani* Slava sits and listens to her, ignoring even the ring of the telephone or the whistle of a tea kettle in the middle of an earnest conversation. She'll tell Lesia to sit down and rest her feet, and that's the cue to set aside the broom. *Pani* Slava knows Lesia's marriage is on shaky ground, although she doesn't know any of the particulars; the words had slipped out when Lesia confided she had mixed feelings about returning home.

In retrospect, the knowledge that Lesia was Ostap's second choice seemed to be a warning sign that she'd ignored; a bad omen, like clinking glasses with a spouse during a toast or shaking hands over a threshold. Even now she sometimes wonders if Ostap tells her the truth. Is he still seeing Olya? Is he still inventing excuses to go into Lviv? She's almost asked the boys several times if their father's made any overnight trips, but she's pretty certain the boys would have bragged about being left home on their own.

Not that Lesia's blameless either. She hadn't been bent on anything when she met Mykola at the Ukrainian church festival. Her first impression was of a tall man with a big smile and an even bigger love of cars. He waved his hands around like a Baptist preacher when Lesia got him talking about the Detroit Auto Show, and then he'd burst out laughing at his own gestures. It was just so easy to laugh around Mykola, and they were friends for months before everything changed in one afternoon about five weeks ago. Mykola was free, even if she wasn't, and the crux of it was that he'd made her feel good about herself. Not that it would have taken much to make her feel better in her opinion, but Lesia appreciates the effort all the same. Mykola has been in America for five years and still sends money back to his ex-wife and son in Lviv. That's what she calls commitment.

When she reaches St. Olha's, Lesia wonders if Mykola will attend Mass. He's not a regular churchgoer but Lesia tries to make the service when she can. The church is probably the most familiar place to her in all of America, especially when the choir sings. Those are the moments when Lesia feels as though she's back home, although this church is a lot grander than the wooden

>ne in Vorivka. Services back there are cramped and hot as everyone stands
,houlder to shoulder, but here there are enough pews for everyone to sit in.
_esia likes coming early to look at the colorful murals, but more than that,
,he likes having some time to just sit and let her mind wander. Back when she
ind Ostap were married, the political climate made it too dangerous to have
he service in a church, and she can't help wondering if that had somehow
inxed them too.

Mykola's not inside and Lesia slips into a pew next to Natalya Romankiw,
vho's been living in America for the past two years with an expired visa.
:ven here all Lesia can think about is the letter and how easy it was to get on
i plane and get away from her husband. She barely let Ostap's lips touch her
'ace at the airport, but when the plane dipped during heavy turbulence over
he Atlantic Ocean, Lesia had berated herself for their cold farewell. Right
)efore she left, Ostap told Lesia how he'd run into Olya unexpectedly after
1er husband died, and that she pursued him in the way he'd once pursued
Olya in his youth. Initially, it was almost like he relived the promise of first
ove, he said, until he'd realized how different he'd become in the ensuing
'ears. He also said the affair was far removed from his teenage passion for
Olya. Lesia found it hard to listen to his explanations for the obvious reasons,
:specially given that Ostap was her first love. And anyway, what if he changed
1is mind yet again. It didn't help that he told Lesia he loved her at the end of
his exchange, almost as an afterthought.

When the service ends, Natalya grips her by the elbow as they leave the
church.

"Are you staying then?" Natalya asks.

"Every time I think I've decided, another voice questions everything,"
_esia says. "The boys need me, but they also need a chance for a normal
'uture. Ostap's making next to nothing as a dentist, and we still need to help
)ur parents. My mother told me to stay here for as long as I can, to make sure
he kids have enough money to get university educations. I think she's afraid
he boys will end up stuck in the village with nowhere to go and nothing to
lo and too much vodka around for anyone's good."

Natalya nods. "My mother cried like a baby when I told her I was coming
1ere, but ever since my father got sick, she's been crying at the good fortune
)f having the money to pay for his medicine."

"You can breathe easy, then, knowing you're doing the right thing," Lesia says.

Natalya lets out a snort. "Aah, Leshka. Who said anything about it being easy? You know there's nothing easy about leaving your family behind. Two months, two years, and nothing back there seems to change for the better."

"*Tyho*, Natalya, *tyho*." Lesia puts her arm around the other woman.

* * *

Mykola has a car with an automatic transmission, and when Lesia studied for her license, he taught her how to drive, even urging her to navigate the Detroit freeways, taking her out on Sundays when the roads were free of the weekday rush. At first, Lesia couldn't get over the smoothness of the roads, much less the speed at which everyone zipped along, sometimes with a cell phone plastered to an ear. The road into Vorivka required as much concentration to drive on as it took to hang on to the door in the passenger seat, which is where Lesia always sat when she was lucky enough to get a ride. They were always talking about fixing the road, but it was the kind of talk everyone knew never led to much.

Sometimes Mykola and Lesia drive late in the evening, and Lesia sits in the driver's seat, foot pressed to the gas pedal, whipping up I-75 like she doesn't have a care in the world, like she's 16 years old, and her whole life is uncharted, the future full of unlimited possibilities. They pass by strip malls and movie theaters, even a couple of office buildings made of glass so shiny their reflection reminds her of a sparkling lake buried deep in the Carpathian mountains that she'd seen as a child. Lesia loves the feeling that driving gives her and appreciates how Mykola sits next to her in silence as they ride north for miles, only road and sky ahead, the hum of the wheels pushing them forward. Although Mykola likes to entertain her and will occasionally spend half an hour telling her a detailed joke, Lesia is grateful when he understands this need for her silence. Back home, Ostap found it necessary to coax her out of her quiet moods.

But even Mykola becomes impatient with Lesia these days. Just last week he'd snapped at her in the grocery store when she'd taken too long to select some cheese and crackers. He'd cracked his fingers in the car and wouldn't say a word while she drove home, and she turned the radio up in response.

The problem was that there were too many choices in the grocery store, 30 varieties of cheese alone, she told him later after they'd opened the red wine and were on speaking terms.

"You can't offer up all these choices and expect someone to make a snap decision."

Mykola had nodded but Lesia knew he wasn't happy about the explanation.

* * *

When Lesia and Mykola come together, it's usually after their Sunday drives. Most of the time they go to Mykola's apartment where he prods her into the sofa chair and then cooks dinner as she watches television, enunciating English words aloud while Mykola corrects her from the kitchen. After dinner they end up in the bedroom, and even though Mykola tries to get her to stay the night, Lesia will get up after a few hours and ask him to drive her home. She doesn't want *Pani* Slava to know about her affair although she guesses her landlady has her suspicions.

The affair started when Mykola, who often fixes things for her landlady, stopped by one Sunday afternoon to fix her television set. When Lesia opened the door, she knew her eyes were still red after her argument with Ostap. Mykola didn't say a word about it at first, but after he'd fixed the TV, they sat down at the table. Over *Halka* coffee and poppyseed cookies, Lesia told Mykola more details about her marriage than she'd ever let on to her best friend back home. When she'd walked him to the door, he'd stared at her as if trying to find the right words, then gave up and kissed her right there in the open doorway. Lesia was surprised at how easy it was to let him keep kissing her, and later she could only faintly recall him pushing them back inside the living room and shutting the door.

Tonight starts out like every other Sunday, but when they finished eating, Mykola springs up from the table and hands Lesia a present. She's surprised by the gesture. When she pulls out the road atlas from the wrapping paper, Mykola can hardly contain his glee.

"Isn't it perfect?" he asks. "I could hardly wait to give it to you. I used some of the lottery money."

Still perplexed by the atlas, Lesia shakes her head as Mykola moves toward her and pulls her into an embrace.

"When we're married, I'm going to buy you the fanciest car I can afford, and we're going to drive through every single state in America. We'll just take two weeks off each year and drive and drive," he says.

For a minute Lesia stays wrapped in Mykola's arms. She tries to imagine them driving up and down the highways of America, road maps in the glove

99

box, cameras by their sides. But then all she can think about is how much she liked the butterflies when they'd gone to the conservatory a couple of weeks earlier. Mykola was bored with it all in a few minutes and tugged at her arm, and Lesia had given in and allowed him to pull her along. She thinks about telling him about the butterfly house and how she wanted to chase the butterflies like a little girl, how she was just waiting for one to land on her finger so she could hold it up to her face and feel it rustle its wings. Lesia closes her eyes and hugs Mykola even tighter, kissing him on the side of his neck.

"You're kidding, right?" she finally says, pulling away.

"Don't you want to see America?" Mykola asks, then stops when he sees how pale Lesia has become. "You are going to divorce him?"

Lesia purses her lips, turning away. "I don't know. Maybe. Maybe I will," she says, letting the atlas slip from her fingers to the floor.

* * *

Even though it's almost midnight, Lesia pours herself a cup of tea and then paces around her apartment, opening drawers, closing cupboard doors, even sponging down the microwave oven before she finally turns her attention to the kitchen table. For a moment she's tempted to bake, but then thinks better of it, takes a quick sip of tea and retrieves Ostap's letter from under the pile of newspapers. The phone rings, but Lesia ignores it and instead rips the envelope open, setting the letter down like a bruised peach. Inside she finds an article with a recipe for her walnut *torte* and a note from Ostap.

Moya Doroha,

I hope you don't mind me sending in your recipe to the Trembita newspaper. It won first place in their baking contest, just like I knew it would. I know nothing's ideal, and I can't complain if you really think you're happier now. But I'll be here if you decide you're coming back to me and not just to the boys. I guess I'm still hoping you are coming back in any case.

Ostap

Lesia rereads the note as if expecting a hidden code to spring out if she only looks hard enough. She's not sure if her husband suspects anything or if he just thinks she's happier without him. For a minute Lesia wonders if she's let something slip; a wrong word, an unnatural ring to her voice, or perhaps

100

Ostap has called when she's been at Mykola's. There are too many possibilities to conjure up or perhaps it's nothing at all, but then she looks down at her recipe and smiles at the thought of Ostap digging it out and sending it in for a contest.

Lesia isn't sure if she has any faith in new beginnings or if old hurts can be blown out like a candle or even if new friends can forgive heart-wrenching blunders. All Lesia knows is that if she wants to go on, if there is any forgiveness to be had, both by and for her, she needs to release everything that's wedged inside of her like a cocoon. She gets up and takes a breath, examines the tiny space of her kitchen like it's her life on display, and then she walks to the window overlooking the backyard. There's not much to see here in the dark, especially on a chilly night like tonight, but Lesia pushes up the window as far as she can and leans over so the wind slaps at her eyes. She stands there at the window, enjoying the cold like she's on top of Mount *Hoverlia*, only here there's no breathtaking scenery around, just that feeling you get when you wipe away mist from your eyes, and you can finally see some tracks in the snow ahead of you.

Orange in Bloom

The bird's arrival changed everything. I don't know why it decided to land on my balcony when there are *sotni* of others across Kyiv—most of them with at least a better view of the city, if not the Dnipro River. I live alone on Saksahanskoho Street in the center of the capital, and my balcony overlooks the garbage dump. When Ivan was alive, I'd be on my hands and knees scrubbing it clean, but now I can barely manage with dust overtaking my rooms like the wild mushrooms in the dead zone near Pripyat.

The bird is a scrawny thing yet so full of energy that it hasn't stopped singing during the two hours it's been sitting on top of my bookshelf, a small fluff of green and yellow perched on an old photo of Ivan. It's one of the few good photos I have from when Ivan still had all his curly hair and teeth and before the bullet pierced his left leg during the war and turned him into a cripple. That would have made a lot of men bitter, but my Ivan was the one who knew how to pick up everybody else's spirits.

Anyway, I don't mind the bird sitting there, chattering away, filling up the silence that's usually broken up by the radio. He's got a tuft of white down on the back of his head, like the bald spot Ivan had when he first started losing his hair. I'm guessing this bird's a boy, not by the dark blue on top of his beak, but by the way he's been pecking my fingers ever so lightly. Only a boy would be this gentle to a lonesome widow with too much time on her hands.

My house is never quiet if I can help it, but today I won't turn on the radio or TV. I know there's going to be trouble in the streets sooner or later with the election results being reported one way, as if everything's already been decided, even though most of us know that the voting went the other way. In most countries, a man with a criminal record could never become president. But here in Ukraine, that distinction hasn't stopped the government-appointed

105

nominee. So if I hadn't been sitting on my living room *divan*, listening for sounds of trouble, I never would have heard that bird in the first place. And that's how it all started.

* * *

The streets are quiet, more quiet than usual, or maybe I'm anticipating trouble in the way I often worry about everything. Ivan used to tease me about it—the little quirks I have, like carrying an umbrella in my purse even on sunny days if I wake up with a particular ache in my bones. I can trust my bones better than any weather forecast and being prepared for unexpected events can mean the difference between calamity or a minor inconvenience. That's why I always carry a small flashlight in my pocket, so I can read my newspaper if the power goes out on the metro. It hasn't happened to me yet, but the power's always going off in our building so you can never be too prepared.

I used to carry carrots in my pockets. It gave me something to do when the tram or trolleybus ran late. But now I've switched to sunflower seeds. Easier on the jaw. Seeds are what made me pull out my boots and *kozyh*, made me for a moment at least, forget about the possible dangers outside my front door. I need to provide food and shelter for my new little friend. Of course when I tell my next-door neighbor Svitlana about my plans, she grabs me by the arm and whispers into my ear.

"Troops. At the outskirts of Kyiv. Just waiting for the word to storm the city."

Svitlana is a petite woman, but you wouldn't know it from the mark of her nails on my skin.

"Don't be ridiculous," I say, shaking her off. "You know that a parakeet is a good omen. I'll be back in an hour."

Svitlana is often too dramatic for her own good, but I have to admit a secret part of me is pleased that she'd been astonished, even envious that I'd chosen to ignore her advice and proceed out the door. To be truthful, I was a little uneasy myself, but there's a pet shop not too far away, just around the corner from that overpriced store where they sell fancy toys from Germany.

I walk past the tram stop, my head bent against the wind, the cold pushing me forward with quick steps and for a second, maybe two, I feel like a young girl. A young girl out looking for adventure. A minute later I get more than I bargained for when I hear shouting.

"Look out, Babusia."

A group of boys come flying at me and before I can step away, one of them grabs me around the waist, and I'm spinning around as if we're at a country dance. It's all so quick and frantic that I can't shake him loose, and just when I'm sure we'll both hit the pavement, he lets go. I almost fall then but I'm too busy catching my breath and my balance to yell at him and they're a block away, laughing, before I can muster the words.

"Hooligan. *Bez vyhovannia.* Probably one of those supporters from the Blue camp," I mutter, although I'm not sure of anything anymore.

* * *

We've all been asked to pick between blue and orange as if a color can really identify who you are or what you believe in. I've always been partial to the color blue ever since my mother sewed a beautiful blue dress for my first *yalka* when I was five years old. Orange is loud, obnoxious really, yet when it comes to the election, when it comes to choosing between what has always been or something new, I've got to throw my vote behind this new color I'd never include in my wardrobe. I made up my mind when they poisoned the front-runner and turned his face into a gray mask of pock marks.

To be truthful, though, I probably made that decision a whole lot sooner than that. When my sister Valia's son, Kostyk volunteered to help with the cleanup at the Chornobyl plant, he thought he'd make some good money. He's still alive but he hasn't had one day of good health since that time. I guess you could say it's all connected, or you could say that the front-runner decided to poison himself, but all I'm saying is, I wasn't going to stay home on election day.

* * *

The shop owner's a bit surprised to see me look for a cage while people are gathering on the *Maidan,* readying to protest the elections. I can see him sizing me up as he tells me this, and then he leans over and pats me on the hand.

"Best for you to get home as soon as possible, Babusia. Things can get dangerous very quickly."

For some reason his comment annoys me. The incident with the boys was unpleasant and unexpected, yet now that I'm actually out on the street, I find that I'm a little more curious than afraid.

"I'm not as feeble as you think," I tell him, tightening my grip on the bird cage.

I see him look me over from my worn boots to my plump, lined face, but I straighten my shoulders and stare him down in the same way I talk down the sellers at the Bassarabskiy *bazar*. He shrugs and then laughs, delighted by my response.

"They're setting up tents I hear. Tell them Dyma sent you."

I can still hear him laughing as I leave the warmth of the store behind me. It's about a 15-minute walk, maybe less with the wind pushing me forward, and even though I'm not quite sure what's propelling me on, I realize that I'm not ready to just turn around for home. Not without taking a quick look at what's happening in my own city.

* * *

It's a concert, a music concert, a rock concert, a dizzying blur, fur coats and hats, shoulder to shoulder, orange and orange, splatters of blue, a pilgrimage of sorts, a rally, a protest, flowers and the *militsia* at the sidelines, standing, watching. There must be hundreds, thousands jammed in the square, lining the streets. I feel faint. I feel cold. I feel giddy. I shout "yes!" I shout "yes" to change, "*tak*"... "*tak*"... "*tak*"... until my nose starts streaming, and I taste the tears running down my cheeks. If only Ivan could be standing next to me. There's too many of us, the *militisia* won't fire, won't fire on their own. I stand for moments. I stand for eternity. I stand until I can't feel my toes and remember the bird cage at my feet, the parakeet in my living room. I push through the crowd. I smile at everyone. I smile at a man waving a blue flag. He looks like my Ivan. He scowls back but I know he's watching me. I can feel his gaze on my back. I lift my head up so he can see I feel no fatigue.

* * *

Every day I go back. For the next 17 days until it's over. Sometimes by myself, sometimes with Svitlana. But I don't go empty-handed. The tents the pet shop owner told me about on that first day were no joke. Khreshatyk is no longer a pristine boulevard of shops, restaurants and cafes. Overnight everything's changed. That's where they've set up the tents, and it's where I bring *holubtsi*, *pelmeny*, poppy seed *bulochky*—anything I can prepare. I haven't done this much cooking and baking in years, but there are people here from all over the country with only a few, if any, belongings. Every day there is talk of bloodshed, of troops coming in from the East or even Russia. But surprisingly I sleep more soundly at night than I have in years. I can't even feel the little bumps in my mattress, the pain in my hips. In the mornings, I ing folk songs to my little bird. He likes to sit on my finger and gaze into my eyes like he's about to tell my fortune. I've named him Pomaranchyk, not for his coloring but for the color of the revolution outside. I let him fly around the living room so he can have his freedom. Then after a couple of hours, I pack up all the food I've cooked and head for *Maidan*.

* * *

Siberian cold. Rain. Snow. People and more people. It feels like a nonstop New Year's celebration on the streets of Kyiv. Orange umbrellas, balloons, ponchos. Sometimes there's yelling. Blue flags versus orange scarves. Men bussed in from the eastern regions shouting in our faces, trying to turn the clock back. A few of them are around my age, many much younger, but there's nothing I can say that will change their minds.

I usually head for the orange tents to pass out food, but today I speak to the ones with blue hats and blue ribbons tied on their arms who stop me when they recognize my satchel and realize I'm passing out food. One of them looks like Ivan, the one who scowled at me on my first night on the *Maidan*. Now he grins and bobs his head in recognition. Up close he's not as handsome as Ivan was, but even so he's got nice blue eyes.

"What are you smiling at, old man?" I ask.

He laughs, a hearty sound that catches me off-guard. "You're not going to let an old man starve to death, are you?"

"Didn't they feed you on the bus?"

"No cash or food for me," he says. "Some of the others got money to come here but I got a free bus ride and some vodka." He steps closer and whispers into my ear. "You know I always wanted to see Kyiv. This seemed as good an opportunity as ever."

I can't help laughing at that. I give him a little more food than I originally intended but stop short of doling out the entire bag. I nod at him as I turn away and then hesitate.

"You didn't just come all this way for the scenery, did you?"

"Well," he says, looking around. "It's not so easy to shrug off the threats. Not when your boss is ordering you who to vote for. But in the end—where's the truth?"

I stiffen, although I perfectly understand his feelings and all the confusion and fear behind them. Yet in the past few days, I've come to believe that anything is possible. I want to tell him that he needs to open himself up

109

to each day like he's reliving that first kiss with the girl he's had his eye on for years. That standing and shouting in a square with thousands of people can give you the kind of power that can bring about change. But I don't say anything because there is a line we must all cross on our own.

Instead I take him by the arm and invite him home to tea. I tell him about the parakeet who flew onto my balcony and changed my life. Later we will return to the Maidan, and I hope that he joins me up front near the stage. No matter what happens next, everything has already changed.

About the Author

Ksenia Rychtycka has an M.A. in Creative Writing from Columbia College Chicago. Her short stories and poems have appeared in *The Dalhousie Review*, *The Literary Bohemian*, *Wisconsin Review*, *Alaska Quarterly Review*, *Hubbub*, *Yellow Medicine Review*, *The MacGuffin*, *Santa Fe Literary Review*, *Dunes Review*, and other literary journals and anthologies. She was a featured poet in the Spring/Summer 2011 issue of *River Poets Journal* and a finalist in the 2008 *Blue Mesa Review* Fiction Contest. To learn more about her work, visit kseniarychtycka.com.

Ksenia lives with her husband and daughter in the metro Detroit area and works as a freelance copy editor.

A Conversation with Ksenia Rychtycka

What was the inspiration behind this collection of short stories?

The earliest stories in the collection were started while I was earning my M.A. at Columbia College in Chicago. I grew up in the Detroit Ukrainian-American community and was raised with a very strong sense of that background—for instance I learned to speak English at the age of five, I attended a Saturday Ukrainian-language school, I was involved in a Ukrainian scouting organization, etc. In a sense, it was like growing up in two cultures.

When I went to college and began writing fiction, I purposely avoided using my background in my work. It wasn't until I got to Columbia and a few years had passed that I felt compelled to write about the background that I came from and knew, and that was when my stories really came alive. I started writing this collection around the time the Soviet Union was collapsing and that was also a motivating force. I traveled to Ukraine one year before independence was declared, and then a few years later, I moved to Kyiv for a few years. It was a challenging and exciting time and those experiences also fueled the stories for *Crossing the Border.*

When did you become interested in writing? What writers particularly inspired you?

I've been writing, in one form or another, since I was a child. Books were always a part of my life and both of my parents were Ukrainian writers, so I like to think it's in my genes. My mom is a poet, and my father wrote novels so writing was not a foreign idea in my family.

There have been many writers who have inspired me over the years in different phases of my life. I have always loved Jane Austen, and I always have great pleasure in going back to her novels. Some of the writers who really helped me with my own writing were those who tackled similar cultural issues in their own work. These include Edwidge Danticat, Jhumpa Lahiri, Chitra Banerjee Divakaruni, Yiyun Li, Junot Diaz, and Louise Erdrich. A.S. Byatt, John Fowles, Margaret Atwood, Janice Kulyk Keefer, and Haruki Murakami are also writers I greatly admire.

What surprised you the most during the writing of this collection?

As far as the process of writing is concerned, I didn't realize just how many revisions it would take before I felt that each story, and the collection as a whole, was complete. Sometimes it takes a great amount of time to get the right perspective to tell the story. For instance one of the stories, "Homecoming" was written during my days at Columbia. I set that story aside, and then years later revisited it and ended up rewriting the whole piece from two different points of view. There are only a few paragraphs that remain from the original.

The other surprise was discovering thematic links that I was not conscious of during the writing process. Obviously, the cultural links were very intentional. But when it came time to provide my publisher with input for the book cover I was initially at a loss until I realized after discussion with my husband that birds through the notion of flight or as visual images were present in most of the stories. It was an interesting and very timely discovery!

Some of your stories are set against the backdrop of political happenings in Ukraine. How difficult was it to connect the personal with the political especially for an audience unfamiliar with the country?

At heart I think that we as readers are always interested in the personal. Lives continue in the midst of political upheavals and repressions, and it is those everyday universalities that unite us no matter the country we live in. The lonely woman who crashes strangers' weddings in the Midwest and the elderly woman who ventures out in the midst of a revolution to buy a cage for a lost bird are linked together in ways that transcend culture. I tried to provide some sense of the political reality that my characters were dealing with and obviously the experience of living in Ukraine, working with local people and getting to know the culture on a personal level, was essential in writing some of the stories. So it was a very natural blend.

Why did you choose to end the collection with the 2004 Orange Revolution?

I wanted the book to end on a positive note, during this great moment of possibility for change. Although events in Ukraine have not gone the way many people had hoped, it was still an amazing and breakthrough time. I also had left Ukraine a few years before the Orange Revolution, and I felt that this was a good stopping point and that the stories worked together as a cohesive whole.

What are you working on next?

I'm currently writing poems and have a project in mind about four medieval historical women who were sisters. This may or may not turn into a prose piece.

Glossary

Most of the italicized words used in this story collection are Ukrainian. Origins of other words are indicated below.

argotera (Greek) — see you later
Babtsia, Babusia — grandmother
borsch — beet soup
bez vyhovannia — ill-mannered, coarse
bulochky — rolls
bouzouki (Greek) — long-necked stringed instrument that resembles a mandolin
dacha (Russian) — summer cottage/house
Dido — grandfather
divan — couch
Dobriy dyen — Good day
dolmades (Greek) — Stuffed grape leaves
doroha — dear
Dovbush's skelia — group of natural and man-made structures carved out of rock. The formation is named after an 18th-century local rebel leader named Oleksa Dovbush who became a folk hero and was compared to Robin Hood.
dytynko — child (diminutive form)
fourchette (French origin from the word "fork") — after-party
fryzura — hairdo
Holodomor — artificial famine-genocide imposed on the Ukrainian people in 1932–33 by Stalin's regime
holubtsi — stuffed cabbage rolls
kanapky — sandwiches
KGB — umbrella organization for the premier security agency, secret police and intelligence agency in the Soviet Union

kilim — woven tapestry rug. Traditional Ukrainian kilims have either stylized floral ornamentation or geometric patterns.

kohana — darling

kokardy — hair bows

kopiykas — penny (plural form)

korovai — Ukrainian wedding bread

kozyh — fur winter coat

kvas — a traditional non-alcoholic drink made from rye, fruit and herbs

liznyk — wool coverlet

lyalka — doll

Maidan — Square (referring to Independence Square—*Maidan Nezaleznosty)*

makivnyk — poppy seed roll

medivnyk — honey cake

medivnychky — honey cookies

Metaxa (Greek) — distilled spirit, consisting of a blend of brandy, spices and wine

moussaka (Greek) — eggplant-based layered casserole

Muscat — sweet Crimean wine

Ouzo (Greek) — anise-flavored liqueur

Plaka (Greek) — old historical neighborhood of Athens, located on the north slopes of the Acropolis

Pani — Ms. or Mrs.

pelmeny — small dumplings consisting of seasoned ground meat wrapped in a dough pocket and shaped similarly to tortellini

pomynky — a sit-down meal served after a funeral where family and friends reminisce about the departed

pysanky — Ukrainian Easter eggs that are decorated by using a wax-resist method. The word comes from the verb pysaty, "to write," since the designs are not painted on, but written with beeswax.

pyrizhky — pastry with either a sweet or savory filling

retsina (Greek) — strong white or red wine flavored with pine resin

rosyl — chicken noodle soup

sotni — hundreds

Sovietske Champagnske — generic brand of sparkling wine produced in the Soviet Union

studenets — jellied fish or meat dish

Tato — father

tistochky — cookies
Toh yomoo (Greek) — my boy
tsvibak — yellow holiday bread similar to pound cake
torte — fancy layer cake with rich filling
tyho — quiet
tzatziki (Greek) — cucumber yogurt dip
varenyky — dumplings filled with meat, potatoes, sauerkraut, cheese or fruit. Also called pyrohy.
vokzal — train station
vyshyvka — embroidery
yasoo (Greek) — hello or good-bye
Yiayia (Greek) — grandmother
zabava — formal dance
zembekiko (Greek) — traditional Greek improvisational dance with a rhythmic pattern. Known as an intensely personal dance.

CPSIA information can be obtained
at www.ICGtesting.com
Printed in the USA
BVHW070843110819
555535BV00003B/424/P

9 781939 289018